THE GREENS

A SNOWBOOKS HORROR NOVELLA

Proudly published by Snowbooks

Copyright © 2016 Andrew Hook

Andrew Hook asserts the moral right to be
identified as the author of this work.
All rights reserved.

Snowbooks Ltd.
email: info@snowbooks.com
www.snowbooks.com.

British Library Cataloguing in Publication Data.
A catalogue record for this book is available
from the British Library.

Paperback: 978-1-911390-19-0
Ebook: 978-1-911390-20-6

THE GREENS

Andrew Hook

In an expanding universe, time is on the side of the outcast. Those who once inhabited the suburbs of human contempt find that without changing their address they eventually live in the metropolis.

Quentin Crisp, The Naked Civil Servant

❄

THE CHILDREN

ONE

The fingers of her brother's hand wriggled in her grip, but she had no intention of letting go. The noise came again, a distant tinkling of tiny bells reverberated the cool air. Their sheep were quiet, heads down, aware. She bent her knees and whispered in her brother's ear. He nodded, but she knew he didn't understand. Sometimes she felt she was the only one who understood anything.

Their sun was low in the sky, casting their faces in a sub-orange glow. The landscape here was barren, rocks pushed through the grass, stubbling the distant view. She tugged on her brother's hand, but he was reluctant to move. If the sound of the bells entranced her, then they had hypnotised him. He didn't waver.

She tried to release her fingers but whereas before she had reached for his hand, now it was him who held her tight. She shook her fist, hard, and almost knocked him to the floor. His eyes were a mixture of wonder and fear. The bells continued. When it came to the Unknown, neither of them had any experience. You couldn't rely on rumour.

She whispered again as the sun sank lower, her brother's face taking on a healthy glow. Soon it would be too late, surely. The sun crackled. She tugged again, and as though he were reforming from a petrified version of himself, he stirred.

The bells sounded quite different from those of St Martin's church, and anyway they were in the wrong direction. She had never heard such an insistent, persistent calling before.

Her brother jerked his mute head out of his reverie and pointed in the direction of the sound. When she tilted her head it was a question. He nodded a *yes*.

She looked behind them, towards their village, but it was quiet. The flock would be safe. As one, they began to walk towards the rockier ground, their shoeless feet used to the sharpness of the stones. And as they walked, the sun's power began to wane, coating them in a light of pure syrup.

As they became mere specks in the distance, a few of the sheep bleated. The sound echoed in the canyon.

*

The sides of the canyon began to close in on them as they progressed, as though they were entering a funnel. At times the bells seemed louder, other times further afar. The faint glow that illuminated their way dimmed then heightened. The girl imagined they were making a transition between one place and another, delineations of twilight. Still, despite the potential for fear, she was drawn towards the sound. Fear in her world wasn't a familiar commodity. She felt it only as a faint prickle on the back of her neck.

After a further distance her brother began to tug her hand. The girl knew he was considering the flock. She also knew that they should be at the forefront of her mind. Briefly, a shadow of doubt flickered. What about the elders? Then she shook her head and pressed on.

A light beamed ahead of them, brighter than anything she had previously known. The bells were much louder, inside her head. She squinted, the light radiating her eyelids, making them translucent. She was pulling her brother along now; she could feel his heels digging in the ground.

They were approaching an opening. A series of jagged rocks zigzagged in front of them. Her brother overcame his fear and began climbing. She followed. His body shape obscured her view as they twisted first one way then another. The gaps between the rocks became smaller, just as the light ahead became brighter.

She knew this was wrong.

But she did it anyway.

The bells stopped as they made their final ascent. They collapsed, blinded by the light.

TWO

She was aware of voices, though the language was unfamiliar. Her eyes were closed and she decided not to open them. Through her lids, the intensity of the light she had first experienced had mellowed and was not unlike the shade within her village.

Rugs seemed to be covering her. She was snug, warm. Moving her arms she found that she wasn't bound. She wanted to sleep again, embrace the possibility of dream, but the lure of the voices overrode her senses. Tentatively, she opened her eyes.

Although the light was dim, the first thing she noticed was the colour of their skin. It was pale, with a creamy sheen, quite at odds with that of her village. Instinctively she shrank back. Concern spread across the faces of those around her. She realised that in all appearances other than their skin colour they resembled herself.

She was inside a wooden building, not unlike those in her village. Through slats in the sides she could see some comforting greenery. She was also aware of a small fire, probably behind her. As her eyes became adjusted to the room, they stung from the smoke. The faces did not look unkind, but she could tell that they were curious.

Suddenly she swung her head from side to side, sat up, but was immediately forced down. She couldn't explain her actions, yet she hadn't felt threatened. Those around her appeared protective, calming, concerned. The exertion made her dizzy, the smoke and the light confused her senses, and her soul was bursting inside her body, heading towards the roof. She knew that she was otherwhere, and this awareness drove her to lose consciousness again; her final thoughts being that her brother hadn't been with her in the room.

*

She wasn't sure how long she slept, but when she opened her eyes it was pitch dark; darkness she hadn't experienced before. It wasn't quiet, she could hear murmurings from outside, but again didn't understand the language. A jolt of fear ran through her. Where was she? Where were her family? The memory of the journey slowly came back, but with it there was no understanding. Her stomach ached and she realised she was hungry, but simultaneously felt too sick to eat.

Her past rushed up within her mind and overtook her. A sense of vertigo filled her. A wave of other emotions that she couldn't rationalise swam back and forth in her mind. Instinctively, she began to count.

Once her village rituals were complete she became calm. Despite the warmth of the blankets she sidled out of them. She was dressed as she had been. Tentatively she stood and found her dizziness had passed. She waited a few moments as her eyes adjusted to the darkness. It appeared she was alone in the room. Objects delineated within her vision, and she could see a clear route towards the doorway. Trusting those who had found her, she ventured towards the opening.

A fire was burning outside. Through a gap in the door she could see there were several other huts surrounding hers. She wondered if her brother was inside one of them. A mixed group of people sat around the fire, all ages, both sexes. Their clothes were rough, made of a coarse material. Some were barefoot. A pot bubbled over the fire, and the smell from it made her both hungry and nauseous. She wondered why she was feeling ill. Just how much time had passed since they had emerged into this place?

One of the children looked up and saw her in the shadows. He tugged at what she supposed was his mother's sleeve, his eyes wide. She stood her ground in the doorway, waited to be beckoned towards the fire. The night was cool, she didn't need its heat, but the company would be welcome. She also needed to find her brother.

The child's mother rose from the fire and approached her, a friendly smile on her face. She said a few words that couldn't be understood. The girl shrugged her shoulders, unsure if it was correct to do so. She didn't try to speak, considered that remaining mute might be best for the meantime. The woman took her hand, but instead of leading her towards the fire they made their way across to an adjacent hut. The woman mumbling under her breath as she did so.

The door was pushed open. The girl saw her brother lying on a mattress of straw. She rushed over towards him, took his hand in hers and kissed his face. His skin was hot, feverish. She instantly regretted bringing him here, even though choice had not been an option. His lips were cracked; tiny striations punctuated them like fissures in hardened clay. His eyes flickered, but despite being open she could tell they didn't see.

She became aware of the old woman kneeling down beside her, holding a gourd in one hand. Reaching out towards her brother the girl watched as she poured water out of the gourd and onto his face and lips. He coughed; once, twice; then sat up violently, shaking his head so that droplets of water spun away into the surrounding darkness.

The girl turned her face to the woman and smiled.

Then she turned back to her brother. He opened his mouth so she put a finger to her lips, then pressed her hand down on his forehead. He returned to the straw, closed his eyes, and fell asleep.

The girl sat beside him for a few moments more, then noticed the woman had left and quickly shook him awake.

"What's happening?"

"I'm not sure, how are you feeling?"

Her brother touched his forehead. "Feverish."

"Are you hungry?"

He nodded.

"Me too."

They remained in silence for a while as the girl considered their circumstances. Who could they trust? She was young, she didn't know much of anything at all, but the people they were with seemed welcoming, the old woman in particular. She tried to think about her own family, but blankness slid across the forefront of her mind and shut everything down. No matter, it would come to her in good time. They had shelter and were safe. She lay down beside her brother and whispered assurances in his ear, until eventually she watched him fall back to sleep.

THREE

Morning brought the sound of approaching hooves. Chickens scattered diagonally as the girl watched through the half-open door as the men approached. She had slept fitfully, dreamt little. Her brother was still sleeping, the daylight infusing his greenish skin with an almost luminescent glow.

Three riders dismounted. She couldn't see the old woman of the previous evening. Men from the village talked to the riders, and she saw one of them point towards their hut. Instinctively she ducked down, pretended to sleep, unsure as to whether they brought danger.

Behind her closed eyelids she heard the creak of the wooden door. Opening them slightly she saw the three men watching. Maybe they too spoke a language which she wouldn't understand. She watched as they pointed to their own arms, their own faces. Then one of them seemed to summon up courage to enter the room, and she almost smiled that these strong men seemed cautious in her presence, whilst the villagers of the previous evening had done no more than accept them.

She opened her eyes. Momentarily, the man stepped back.

Then, perhaps wary of how his fear might manifest itself, he stepped forwards again.

She stood. She was perhaps two-thirds of his height. For a while they regarded each other, then the man opened his mouth and laughed, breaking the tension. He turned to the other men, said something again, but the girl continued to stand, protective of her brother.

The man glanced to the boy on the floor, who had now also woken but didn't rise. Then he extended his hand to the girl.

She didn't know what to do. Then, behind the men in the doorway, she noticed the old woman was standing near the back of a group of villagers. The woman smiled, nodded in encouragement, and the girl took the man's hand, his fingers hard as twigs against her own delicate skin.

Again, the man turned and said something to the group. Another man entered, bent down and touched the boy's forehead, then pushed his arms underneath him, lifted him, and began to carry him outside.

The girl could feel the fingers holding her hand tighten their grip, then she too was led outside.

She squinted against the bright sun. She heard her brother sob. In daylight, the differences between the colours of their skin were much more evident. The villagers and those of the horsemen were almost white, little more than a soft pink. Only hers and her brothers were a natural green.

Hunger pangs bit her stomach. She turned around. A small crowd had gathered. Some younger men seemed to be arguing, expressing anger. Others were smiling, but their faces were equally confused. She scanned the crowd, looking for the familiar face of the old woman, and saw that she now advanced, carrying a woven basket. The woman's fingers reached into it and pulled something out, offered it to her, pointed at her mouth. She sniffed, then pushed it aside. It was brown, a lump of something she couldn't distinguish. The woman offered the basket itself this time, and she rifled around inside. Nothing seemed edible, and she pushed the basket away.

The man holding her hand knelt beside her. Spoke words which had no meaning. Then he stood again, conversed with the rest of the villagers. Her brother was still crying, but she recognised the sound and it was borne of hunger rather than fear.

Eventually, a decision seemed to have been reached. She was led towards one of the horses and lifted astride it, as the man hoisted himself up and over to sit behind her. She watched as her brother was handed towards another of the riders who had already mounted. Then all three turned on their heels, and trotted away from the village.

She felt sad, but not fearful. She wondered whether she was trapped within a dream. A feeling swelled up inside her with the promise of adventure. She counted the footfalls within her head, regarded the horses who seemed no different from those in her own village, and watched as they traversed dirt roads across the fields, dried mud flicking up under the hooves, and headed towards a larger complex of buildings which stood close by on a hill.

The men conversed between themselves as they rode, but didn't attempt to engage with herself or her brother. She still had not spoken in the presence of these people, again something within her suggested it would be best to appear mute. She wished she had mentioned this to her brother the previous evening, but their situation had been too strange to think clearly enough to do so.

Greenery assaulted her eyes, her nose. Fields stretched into the distance, trees much larger than those at home extended leafy branches into the sky. The sky! She gasped as she looked upwards, at the palest blue she had ever seen which stretched beyond all possible imagining. This was so different from the twilight world she had been used to. Unable to control herself and the sudden sense of loss, she sobbed until they reached the gates of their destination.

FOUR

She knew this was an important abode: the horses, the gates, the market within the walls. She watched as the inhabitants turned their heads and stared. She sensed hostility here, more so than within the village, but perhaps not personal malice, more a general fear of the unknown.

The Unknown. Isn't that how they came to be here? Once again she remembered the sound of the beckoning bells, the vague warnings she could barely recollect against the unusual. But, in her young mind, how could she differentiate the unusual from that which she simply had yet to experience? Ultimately, they had no more control over their destination than anyone else did.

The market was busy. Various foodstuffs dominated the displays. She saw large orange-coloured vegetables, their surfaces rucked and pitted, smaller but still fat tuber-like structures that reminded her of tree roots, and thinner greenish objects that she thought she recognised.

The pangs in her stomach echoed in her head.

She turned in her seat, and whilst the angle didn't allow her to see the rider's face, she managed to capture his attention as she pointed over to the stalls.

The rider called out to the others and the tiny procession halted. Dismounting, he pulled her from the saddle, and led her over to one of the stalls. Close-up, she recognised the vegetable: a long, slightly furred green item which, as she picked it up and split it along its length, spilled out smaller oval substances. Greedily, she placed them in her mouth.

They were delicious. She reached out for more, but the stallholder grabbed her hand and held it tight. An altercation occurred between the rider and the man, then she saw metal changing hands and the grip was released. The rider scooped up several of the green vegetables and passed them to her, turning around he shouted a word which sounded like *beans* to the other riders, then walked up to the mount containing her brother and passed some of them up.

Beans. They were fresh in her mouth, and she ate greedily. They weren't exactly the same as those in her village, but minor taste differences didn't matter. She continued eating until her hands were empty and a slew of green carcasses littered the floor. Glancing at her brother she saw that he was also eating, although much slower, his movements lethargic, his jaw slack.

Again, she was lifted onto the horse and they completed the rest of the journey, weaving along a track that led through a series of alleyways until finally they stopped before the much more impressive house on the hill.

Dismounting, they walked to the entrance, her brother carried by one of the riders. An overall feeling of dread pervaded her senses. Not necessarily of the situation they were in, but a creeping awareness that they might never return to the land from which they had come.

They were hustled inside. She had never seen such an opulent interior. The furnishings appeared plush, well fed dogs lazed on richly patterned carpets, objects seemingly for ornamentation with little practical value dotted the room. She had heard of similar residences outside of her own village, but had never thought she would see such luxury. She watched as her brother was laid on a soft extended chair, then waited with the riders for someone to come.

Minutes passed. She began to feel hungry again, craved more of the beans. Her brother still held a few in his hand, but he wasn't attempting to eat them. Again, that dread seeped through her. What if he were ill and didn't recover? Was she destined to spend the rest of her life here, alone with these strangely-coloured people?

She saw the dogs prick up their ears long before she saw or heard their master. He descended a stairway towards the back of the room. Long boots, nicely tailored, his hair swept back from a rather stern face which mellowed as he saw her, then frowned as his eyes glanced over at her brother.

He spoke to the riders as he advanced, then dropped to crouch before her. A hand touched her cheek, whether in tenderness or wonderment at her skin she couldn't tell. When he spoke she could smell something rich on his breath, but his words were just as unintelligible as ever. Suddenly he prised open her mouth, as if he were looking to find no tongue. His fingers felt soft. Having satisfied himself he pointed towards his body and spoke again: *Richard de Calne.*

She had no idea what it meant.

FIVE

She came to know more over the following months. Richard was the local landowner. She was told this meant he was wealthy, but it took a while to understand the term. For amusement he had sent for them after having heard of their arrival. His knowledge sated, they were despatched to the servants' quarters, living in a small hot room at the back of the house, regarded suspiciously by some, and benevolently by others. During this time, her brother's condition worsened.

Not having had names they were provided them. She wore hers, Agnes, like a badge. Naming her had given her an identity. Her brother, Charles, never came to understand his. After a month, he had died.

His absence hit her hard. Three days of crying, of loneliness and desperation, tormented her soul. Then came the guilt. Surely she should have resisted the pull of the bells, being an older sibling. Had he not tried to wriggle away from her? She couldn't determine the cause of his ailment. Whilst she had been quizzed about their time underground, and examined in a multitude of ways, she could only confirm that he had been healthy in their world, but somehow not in theirs.

In theirs. She had learnt some language quickly, becoming almost fluent in a short space of time. One of the servants told her they had been found near the village of Woolpit, wandering and crying, although her memory of this was false. The village was contained in Suffolk, which in turn was contained in England. This much she understood. For a while, until he became distant, Richard de Calne had taken on the role of guardian, but over the days her skin colour had faded, become like those who now resided around her, and with it his interest subsided. Once he had taken her to the village where they had first been found, but the entrance to St Martins could not be located.

She shrugged off rumours of witchcraft. She described the churches in her world, as memory gradually returned to her, and in this gained respect, and sometimes admiration. She told of their twilight existence, their subdued sun, their animals and their lifestyle. But other than generalities, the exact knowledge of her people was blocked to her. She couldn't recall that information.

In her quiet moments, she counted according to her rituals. She calmed herself in incantation.

Gradually her eating habits changed. The beans that had seemed so nourishing continued to be the mainstay of her diet, but other raw vegetables supplemented and improved it with a mixture of flavours. Occasionally she was offered meat, and whilst she didn't always enjoy it, she didn't turn it away. In her world she had the feeling that meat was reserved for the older population, but it was a vague memory and she was content with local custom. After all, there was no indication that she would be able to return.

Her brother was given a burial she did not understand, other than that Richard de Calne had arranged it and that the servants thought it satisfactory.

Whilst examining her brother, the physician had also called on her. According to him, she was eight years old, her brother had been five. These numbers meant little to her, but she accepted them, remembered them, and kept them inside her. He had suggested her skin colour might be attributed to the beans, and if he hadn't looked so serious she would have laughed. The fact was, the beans were familiar food, but in her country they ate a wider variety of vegetables than she had seen in her time in this world. Not all of them were as green as her skin.

She was pleased they had been satisfied with the explanations of her world. She had given herself freely, told all that she knew, and hoped for clemency because of that.

So, what had she remembered? That she was from St Martin's Land with its glorious churches and perpetual sun. That to her knowledge this land must be within her new land, and that she was unaware of this outer existence until it was shown to her. That she had no real idea why she was there.

The only information she withheld were her rituals, her counting, her placing of important objects. These were the secret things, the necessities, her essentials.

She had asked about the bells, the sounds both she and Charles had heard which drew them out of the earth, but had met with confusion. It seemed to be one mystery that would never be solved.

JULIA

ONE

Julia checked and re-checked the seatbelts.

"We're fine, Mummy, we really are."

Holly was growing impatient, but she couldn't be rushed. Everything had to be certain.

"Let me make sure one more time."

Julia checked that Poppy was secured in her carrycot, that this in itself was strapped tight against the backseat. She hated taking the baby in the car, but there wasn't much of an option when the school wasn't within walking distance. Well, it wasn't too far, but Holly often refused point blank to walk, and she wasn't going to risk those accusing eyes that accompanied her every time Holly had one of her screaming fits. She wouldn't pander to her child, and in any event Holly had calmed down considerably since the birth of Poppy, but there did come a point where discretion took over. No doubt Holly saw that as getting her own way. Julia preferred to think that she was in control.

"Come on, Mummy, come on!"

Julia checked the seatbelts again, then slammed the door closed.

Oh my god!

She wrenched it open again, convinced that she had caught one of Holly's fingers. But no, there she was, perfectly okay, with a simple, puzzled look on her face.

"Are you ok, Mummy?"

Poppy gurgled.

Julia smiled. "Yes, I'm ok. Will you do something for me darling?

Will you put your hands in the air and see if you can touch the roof of the car."

"Mum!"

Julia bit her lip. "Just try. Go on, see if you can do it."

Holly reached her hands towards the white canvas of the underside of the roof, and as she did so Julia closed the door as softly yet as firmly as was required. This time, the overwhelming belief that she had harmed Holly had passed. Getting into the front seat, she smiled across to her daughter in the back.

"That's very good, Holly. You can put your hands down now."

"I couldn't reach, Mummy."

"I expect you will when you get older."

Julia turned on the ignition and gravel crunched underneath the wheels of the car as they pulled out of the drive. They'd be late now, unless she put her foot down. And what were the chances of that happening. None, of course.

She took three deep breaths in quick succession. Then took them again. Then again. Done.

Without hesitation she drove towards the centre of town. There was much to do when she returned home, and she really couldn't waste a moment longer.

TWO

"Are you okay?"

Richard touched Julia's shoulder as they lay in bed. She didn't respond, he could feel her drawing away from him.

"I'm fine. I'm tired, that's all."

"We've hardly spoken this evening."

She turned to face him. "Well, what do you expect? You were on the computer as soon as you had your dinner. I don't enjoy talking to your back, you know."

"I was researching your family history. You know how important that is to me."

"I hear that genealogy websites are second in popularity to porno sites."

"What's that supposed to mean?"

"Nothing." Julia bent her head forwards and kissed his mouth. "I'm tired, I told you that. Can't think straight."

Richard lay on his back. "We're ok, aren't we?"

She rested her arm over his chest, gave him a squeeze. "Of course we are. It's the children, isn't it? Little vampires sucking the life out of us."

"That's a nice way to put it."

"And accurate."

"I always knew that children would age me. They grow up so fast, your own life gets forgotten."

"Whatever it might be."

"Hmmm."

Julia pulled back the bedclothes and rested her feet on the carpeted floor. The clock on the bedside table indicated it was nearly midnight. She got up.

"Where are you going?"

"Just want to check on the girls. Get a glass of water too, perhaps. Do you want one?"

Richard rolled over, pulled the sheets up over his head. She couldn't quite hear his muffled reply, but she didn't have to. Shrugging, she slipped on her dressing gown and made her way quietly out of the bedroom.

Across the landing the door to the girls' room was ajar. She caught her breath. Had she left it like that, or had Richard popped his head in before they went to bed? She glanced across to the safety gate at the top of the stairs, but it looked secure. Then she slipped into the bedroom.

She could hear breathing, probably Holly's. That was a good sign. The light on the baby monitor by Poppy's cot was quite clear in the darkness, so the batteries should be working ok. Julia stood by the side of the cot. Poppy was sound asleep. She looked quite angelic in the glow from her night light, but Julia imagined that was how all mothers viewed their offspring. She allowed herself a smile: angels rather than vampires.

Checking that Poppy's blanket was away from her face, she ensured Holly was breathing ok before leaving the room. The girls were fine. Perfectly safe in fact. But still there were things that needed to be done to ensure that remained so.

She unlatched the childproof gate, then checked that it was closed three separate times before making her way downstairs. In the kitchen she poured herself a glass of cold water. She couldn't make up her mind about the quality since the water purifier had been installed. There was definitely a fresh taste to be had, but did the process add hidden impurities as well as taking them away? She tried not to worry.

In the living room she opened the glass cabinet that contained her collection of Lalique crystal. They hadn't been moved, but there was a faint, almost imperceptible, layer of dust that had gathered since yesterday evening. Taking a duster from the adjacent cabinet she deftly moved it around the figures, trying not to disturb them. Almost done, she removed her hand from the cabinet when a corner of the duster dropped, clipping the left wing of the crystal green dragonfly. She caught her breath as it moved a fraction of an inch. Something tightened, and her head began to spin.

One. One two three. Two. One two three. Three. One two three.
One. One two three. Two. One two three. Three. One two three.
One. One two three. Two. One two three. Three. One two three.

She whispered the numbers under her breath, then held it. The house was quiet. Nothing untoward had happened. She looked at the green dragonfly. It hadn't shifted too far out of its position, but it might take a while to rectify it. The other figures, the starfish, butterfly, Bengal tiger, the coloured pieces and the clear, they all seemed to have remained motionless. Taking great care, she slowly moved her fingers towards the dragonfly, and gently nudging it at the base, attempted to replace it in its optimum position.

There. Sitting back she took another look, but it didn't feel quite right. She leant forwards and nudged it again, an infinitesimal fraction to the left. Still it didn't look perfect. She made another attempt. No, not yet. Then another. She took a deep breath. It was becoming increasingly difficult. Her hands began to shake. The whorls in the carpet began to spin. She lay down, stared upwards, imagined watching her darlings through a transparent ceiling. It was no good, she would have to continue.

She was exhausted.

She tried again.

One two three, one two three, one two three.

Richard was in a deep sleep by the time she climbed into bed. But it was all alright. Everything was fine. The protections were in place.

She was asleep before she heard the second chime of the clock at three in the morning.

*

"Mummy!"

Holly jumped on the bed. Julia tried to open her eyes but fresh sticky sand sealed them. She flung out an arm. No Richard. He must be up. Holly burrowed underneath the covers. Her daughter's feet were cold. Julia snuggled against her. Smelt the intense child aroma that came from freshly washed pyjamas and slept-in skin. Safe. She was perfectly safe, and loving, and good. Julia breathed a sigh of relief.

Rubbing the sleepy out of her eyes she glanced at the clock on the bedside table. Nearly seven already. Richard would be downstairs, feeding Poppy. She could trust him with that. He was a good father. Everything this morning seemed bright and safe.

Holly's arm around her was suffused with need. She kissed her on the cheek and received another hug. All the worries of motherhood were worth it. She kissed her again, then eased away from her daughter and out of bed. Taking the cord of Holly's dressing gown out from the wardrobe, she slipped it through the loops and tied it tight around her daughter's body.

"Have you had breakfast yet?"

She could smell fresh toast on the grill downstairs.

"Not yet Mummy. Can I have Frosties, Mummy? Can I have Frosties, please?"

She nodded. She wasn't keen on the sugar content, but she wanted a filling breakfast inside her daughter and some days whatever did the trick was best. Keeping close to her, she followed Holly downstairs where Richard was in the kitchen. Poppy was sitting in her high chair, safely strapped in, her face covered in pulped Weetabix.

"Sleep well?" Richard was at the breakfast bar, adding blackcurrant jam to slices of toast. "I didn't hear you come back to bed."

"You were fast asleep," Julia smiled. She reached into a cupboard and pulled out the box of Frosties. In the corner of her eye she saw Holly clamber onto her chair at the table. "How about you? Did you sleep well?"

Richard nodded. He had awoken during the night to find that Julia wasn't in bed. But that wasn't unusual, she didn't need as much sleep as he did.

Julia bit into her toast. "Are you opening up tomorrow?"

Richard nodded. Before the season was in full swing he often refrained from opening the shop on Thursdays. It was his Saturday in the week, as he liked to call it. It was also the one day that he and Julia could spend some time together without Holly forcing herself on them, although Poppy's birth had added an extra complication to the equation.

"The weather's hotting up. You can feel it in the air. Looks like the summer season might be starting early."

Julia shrugged. "It's not as though we need the money."

"Maybe not, but if I close on too many days it'll send out the wrong signals."

They ate the rest of their breakfast in silence, watching Holly crunch on her cereal, milk running down the corners of her mouth.

THREE

After she had dropped Holly off at school Julia returned home and placed Poppy in her cot. She tended to sleep intermittently during the day. As well as making certain the baby monitor was working, Julia would check on her regularly, ensuring that her blanket was away from her face, that she wasn't lying in a difficult position, that her breathing was ok. Even a sleeping baby was a full-time job.

Away from the child she cleaned the house from top to bottom. Starting with her bedroom she stripped then remade the bed: perfect four corners and plumped up pillows. Taking out the tape measure that she kept in her bedside cabinet, she checked the distance of the curtains from the window frame three times. Satisfied, she looked in on Poppy before entering the bathroom.

Richard had been messy with the toothpaste, a hunk of white blocked the plughole and frothed the surrounding area. Sighing she swirled it with hot water, the paste getting smaller and smaller until it eventually plopped through the grid. She squirted cleaning fluid around the ceramic basin and the taps, then polished until she could see her distorted face in them. Finally, she turned each tap so that the *H* and *C* letters were perfectly aligned, facing her as would the letters on a keyboard.

Again, she checked on Poppy, decided to sit beside her for a while. Her skin looked rosy soft in the half-light. Julia bent over the cot, smelled her in, gently kissed her on the cheek. A small sigh escaped from Poppy's mouth, the barest breadth of a breath, then her breathing regulated itself again. Warmth spread up through Julia's body. She knew she was a good mother, a careful and attentive mother, and it was in the quiet times such as these that all her work came to fruition.

She left the room and went downstairs, intending to start her cleaning there. Occasionally she felt lonely in this house. They hadn't really made any friends since they moved to Southwold. It wasn't that Suffolk people were any less friendly than those neighbours she had before, only that their ties had already been established and as newcomers they found it difficult to slide their way in. Most of the surrounding houses were lived in by locals, who had grown up together and gone to the same schools. This was a small town, there was no larger community, and since her parents death she didn't really have anyone to turn to.

Plus, of course, her secrets couldn't be divulged to anyone. Her mother had made that patently clear otherwise all their work might be undone.

She didn't know much about her extended family. Both her parents had been quiet on the subject, and she had the assumption there was some family history that they didn't want to be revealed. She was fine with that. She had never known her grandparents, except on her father's side, and whilst they had been nice they hadn't played a great part in her life. With Richard, things were different. She knew he had a mini-obsession with ancestry that seemed tailor-made to compliment his antiques business, and his history had been researched as far back as it could. She supposed she should grant him this one peccadillo, however it ate into so much of their time that she was never happy when he was on the computer.

Surely life was for the living after all?

Of course, he had started to root about in her past shortly after they had got married. She found it slightly distasteful, as though he were searching for the dark secret that everyone else had been hiding. But really she knew there was no such secret, other than her rituals, and had insisted that so long as he didn't bother her with any details he could go back as far as he liked.

Unless, of course, he came up with something so shocking that she had to be informed. She had laughed as she said this, not really expecting him to find anything, and, so far, he hadn't.

She opened her Lalique cabinet and was relieved to see that her items had not been disturbed nor did they need dusting. It was these that she was most particular with, her little guardians. Whilst her rational mind sometimes fought against the notion that such protections were necessary — God knows she had seen enough television programmes debunking her concerns — she knew deep inside that they were not to be trivialised. And come the time that Holly grew old enough to understand this, she would pass the baton onto her to carry on.

She finished cleaning the remainder of the house, checked that the armchairs were resting correctly, their feet central to the little wooden coasters they resided in, the worn parts hidden from view. In the kitchen she bleached the surfaces, then began to prepare a meal for Poppy. She was almost six months old and starting on solids, so she chopped a few vegetables, blended them, and ended up with green mulch that looked disgusting but which she knew would be nutritious.

Heading back upstairs she sat again watching her child, gently popping Poppy's thumb out of her mouth, her heart in her own throat as she waited for her next breath. When it came, she also released hers. Then breathed in and out twice more. Finally, she reached into the cot and cradled her daughter, heading downstairs as Poppy woke and reassuringly cried.

FOUR

She spent the early evening playing with her daughters. Once again, Richard seemed glued to his computer, and she occasionally glanced over in his direction to check the sites he was visiting. Not that she suspected anything underhand, but she just wanted reassurance that he was doing something rather than sitting there and avoiding fatherly responsibilities. She knew he would have preferred a boy for a second child, but boys didn't run in her family — figuratively or literally.

In a way, she wondered if this, together with his ancestry interests, was what had spurred the search for hers. Her mother had told her there had been no sons for several generations, but there was nothing to back this up. No old photographs, no family members. Perhaps if he was able to see evidence of a male line then it would ring the bell of hope for him, not that Julia wanted more children. It was too much of a worry.

Holly was gentle with Poppy and she was glad of it. The fascination was still there, sibling rivalry had yet to sneak its way into her system and hopefully it never would. She had enough to be concerned about without Holly threatening Poppy, however mild that might be. There were newspaper reports, weren't there, of families whose children had turned on each other, even at an early age. Like cuckoos turfing other birds out of the nest, a steady fight for survival.

Cuckoos implied other families of course. At least she had the satisfaction of knowing both her children were theirs.

She wasn't a snob, but multi-child families with multi-fathers weren't an ideal. She wasn't religious either, but the pull of

Christian values held significance in a commonsense way. It was something she had initially fought against in her teenage years, but rebellion was all part of the fabric of human existence. Looking at Holly tickling Poppy under the chin, she wondered how *their* rebellion would manifest itself.

Whatever happened, she would ensure they were safe, they only had her to rely on.

She looked at the time and decided Poppy should be in bed. Holly sat on the sofa watching cartoons whilst Julia fed the younger daughter. Richard stayed put at the computer. She could see reams of data running up the inside of his glasses, reflected off the screen.

"I'm taking Poppy to bed, keep an eye on Holly won't you?"

He stood up and gave Poppy a goodnight kiss. "Of course I will."

She cradled Poppy close to her breast as she ascended the stairs. Wary of tripping, she counted to three as she reached each step. Her focussed mind ensured there were no accidents, and by the time she had laid Poppy in the cot she felt assured and relieved.

Poppy had started to sleep with her head on her shoulder, but as soon as she touched the cot mattress it was as though she had been placed on broken glass. An ear-splitting cry formed from her tiny mouth, and it took Julia several minutes to placate her, soothing, caressing, whispering, keeping her close. Finally, checking she was asleep and breathing naturally, her sweet pink blanket away from her mouth, Julia turned on the night light and baby monitor and headed back downstairs.

Richard started talking animatedly to her as soon as she reached the living room, jabbering away and pointing at the screen, but the rising panic in her chest was all Julia could think of because Holly was nowhere to be seen.

"Where is she?"

"Who?"

"Holly!"

Richard looked around, the initial worry across his face changing to guilt. Julia knew he was less concerned about the children than she was, and a blaze of anger coursed through every fibre of her being. But there was no time for arguments now, she took a quick glance behind the sofa and then headed into the kitchen, aware of Richard following meekly behind, a sheepish kitten rather than an anxious father.

Holly wasn't in the kitchen, but Julia heard water running in the downstairs bathroom and quickly wrenched open the door. Steam exited the room like wraiths. To her dismay Holly was in the bath, and she snatched her out of the water in terror. Holly's body was warm, an ideal temperature in fact, but this did not assuage her fears of either scalding or drowning. She turned to face Richard in the corridor, but words failed her and she closed the door on him. The whiteness of the wood blanking his face, wiping her anger.

She hugged Holly tight.

"Mum!"

Then through gritted teeth. "Don't ever, *ever*, do that again."

Holly started sobbing, but Julia didn't let go. She counted under her breath.

One. One two three. Two. One two three. Three. One two three.
One. One two three. Two. One two three. Three. One two three.
One. One two three. Two. One two three. Three. One two three.

She felt herself calm down, and as she did so did Holly. She realised in the last of the count that Holly was copying, and this jolted her into tears that ran down her face. Holly's nose was snot-streaked, her hair matted.

She placed her daughter down on the soft bath rug, then dipped her hand in the water. The temperature was perfect.

"I know you were only trying to help Mummy," she said, keeping her voice level, "but the water can get very very hot, and either Daddy or me must be in here with you when you bath. It can be dangerous, ok?"

Holly nodded. Julia could see tears on the verge of spilling again, so she picked her up and plonked her in the water, splashed her face, and spent the next twenty minutes playing with her, encouraging Holly's half-hearted attempts to wash.

FIVE

After Holly had gone to bed, and all her checks had been performed, Julia sat down in an armchair facing the blank television and sighed.

Richard was still at the computer. She could tell he wanted to turn around, tell her how upset he was, but she didn't feel like acknowledging it. She also knew he was bursting to tell her whatever he had found on the pc, but she didn't want to listen. Whatever it was had absorbed his attention to the extent that he had neglected her daughter. She couldn't forgive him for the moment over that, or to have interest in what it was that had engaged him.

It wasn't simply a matter of a mother's concern. It ran deeper than that, although instinctual rather than backed up with hard fact. However, knowing that Holly had been counting with her added to her sense of increasing ease, and after thirty minutes of silence she decided to re-engage with Richard. She did love him, after all.

She rose from the sofa and stood behind him, placing her arms around his neck and resting her chin on his shoulder.

"What you got?"

She could feel the excitement trembling through him, mixed with the relief that she was talking again.

"I've traced your family back to this area. We're in the late 1500's now. That's an incredible time to go back to considering parish registers of baptisms, marriages and burials have only been kept since 1538. I'm unlikely to be able to do much more research on here, but now it's local I might be able to make some enquiries in the surrounding area."

She tried to hide her indifference. "That's lovely, Richard."

He took his hands off the keyboard and held hers. "I'm sorry about earlier, I thought she was behind me."

"Let's forget about it shall we? It's all done and dusted now."

Richard always forgot things faster than she did. In a moment he was back on the ancestry site, pointing out some details she wasn't really concerned with, then pulling up the family tree he had been creating in a Word file. Names and arrows darted across her vision. She supposed she should have been fascinated, but she was indifferent to knowledge of her family and her past. Why that should be so she didn't know.

"Did you notice," Richard said, "that there is no male line in your family? None at all?"

She'd realised that but allowed him his moment of knowledge.

"It all went by too fast for me."

He scrolled back up and down again. "See, all the children have been daughters. This is why it's been hard for me to trace your family. There's been no recurring male surname as far back as I can go — apart from those daughters who remained unmarried of course. Not that there were many of those."

"That sounds a little unusual, doesn't it?"

"Damn right!"

His enthusiasm waned and she felt his shoulders slump under her grip. She knew what that meant for him. There would be no continuation of his name either, and he was the last of the male line in his own family.

She kissed his cheek, worked her fingers down through his shirt and gently stroked his chest.

Maybe she had been too hard on him recently. But life was proving to be such a strain.

He turned to kiss her, catching the edge of his glasses against her nose. She removed them.

"Now I can't see you."

"More fun that way!" She brushed her lips against his mouth, kissed along his cheek, and then breathed softly into his ear. She watched as goosebumps populated his left arm, whilst the right remained as it had been. She loved doing that. She knew his left leg would be goosebumped too.

He swung his chair round and she sat on his lap. They didn't often have time together any more, evenings tended to fly by, and now it was getting close to summer and he would be opening up shop on Thursdays they wouldn't have their midweek tryst either. That was when Poppy had been conceived, a couple of winters ago, she could even pinpoint the exact day.

As she snuggled into his warmth she suddenly heard Poppy crying on the monitor. Within seconds she was racing up the stairs, hearing the creak of Richard's chair as he turned to face the computer once again.

*

That night they made love before she checked on the children and her figurines again. She used the pretence of flushing the condom down the toilet as an excuse to get out of bed, knowing that his endorphins would kick in and he would be fast asleep before her expected return. The house was deathly quiet, but nothing was too quiet for her.

Opening the cabinet she saw immediately that the figures had been moved. The Bengal tiger was face on, instead of side on. And the butterfly was on the right side of the tiger rather than the left. She felt her heart thud, sickeningly, in her stomach. Whilst there had been slight differentiations previously, this was the first time a movement had been so obvious. Briefly, thoughts of Holly, Richard, or even Poppy making the transfer flitted across her mind, but then just as quickly she dismissed them. This was something other, this was the Unknown.

She tried to steady her hands as she picked up the figurines. She gave them a quick polish, holding them separately in case one should knock into the other. Heaven forbid she should chip one. Before she returned them, she gave the figures at the back a thorough examination, in case the changes at the front had been a diversion, but everything else seemed to be in place.

She completed her breathing and counting rituals, then replaced the tiger and the butterfly, their positions in the cabinet etched into her mind as precisely as if they were outlined in chalk. Once positioned, she tapped them gently with her fingernail, until she was perfectly sure they were exact. Then she stopped and realised that her forehead was wet. She glanced at the time, already it was past two o'clock.

The room was chilly, the approaching summer had yet to infuse the house with warmth lasting into the evening. She curled up on the sofa, considered turning on the television to distract the thoughts running through her head, but decided against it. Maybe she had to tackle those thoughts head on.

She had been aware of a presence at the periphery of her consciousness for some time. Not only since her mother had described the rituals, or at least, how certain rituals had to be individually applied, but more recently, particularly since Poppy had been born. Just a nagging sensation at the back of her mind, spurring her on sometimes, but occasionally arguing against her, suggesting that her rituals had no actual importance. She had blocked those thoughts out, tradition was a powerful thing and she couldn't — wouldn't — be swayed otherwise. Now it seemed those forces were finding other ways to corrupt her customs.

She sighed. Again she looked at the ceiling and could envisage her children lying safe in their beds, protected for one more night, but for how long after that. Her head began to hurt.

She tried to distract herself, thought of Richard's findings. It crossed her mind that mothers tend to be more protective of children, that might explain the predomination of the female line in her ancestry, but at the same time she knew it was nonsense. Even if there were connections to her past, surely they couldn't go back that far?

Richard had asked for her permission to contact some of the family he had already traced. She wasn't certain what good that would do, but then she had to remind herself he was interested in the history of her family only, not beyond that. She allowed herself a smile as she realised how different they were as partners, and yet they gelled together all the same. Initially she had said no, but in the morning she decided she should to allow him his interest. Apparently there was a website where he could make his enquiries without needing to give out personal details, and that sounded fine to her. However under no circumstances did she want to be traced, even if she was not one hundred percent sure why.

SIX

She slept fitfully; her dreams cloaked in green, as though seen through a coloured sweet wrapper or watched through her Freeview box which intermittently malfunctioned.

She was under a pale sun, with evening seemingly approaching. Holly was walking alongside her, holding her hand tight. She became aware that they were heading towards school, and she vaguely wondered why they were approaching on foot. Ahead of them the path was deserted, it seemed much too late to be going that way. But there was enough reality in the dream for her to realise it was just that, and like many dream-states the discrepancy floated away from her.

Holly pointed up ahead, towards a small white mass by the school gate.

"Is that snow, Mummy?"

She knew it couldn't be. They were approaching summer after all, but she decided to play along.

"It could be, Holly."

They walked closer. It soon became obvious it wasn't snow, but a white polythene bag, weighed down by water into peaks and troughs. She looked down at the path and realised it was wet. It must have rained overnight.

"It's a bag," Holly said.

"Not a bag," she responded quickly, "it's a portal to the lost world of Zordan. If you step on the bag, you'll descend to an underground city."

Holly laughed and she smiled.

"If you go," Holly said, "then you'd be a legend. Although I won't tell anyone."

"Then I wouldn't be a legend," she said.

They were almost at the bag now. A shop label could be seen on the underside.

"See Mummy, it *is* a bag!"

She nodded, then was horrified as Holly jumped onto the bag and disappeared into the bowels of the earth with a squeal.

She stamped on the bag quickly, water leapt off it and soaked the bottom of her trousers. The ground underneath was hard.

As she awoke, she heard Holly's voice ringing in her ears. "Mummy, I'm going to be a legend!"

*

As promised, Richard went into work that day, opening up the shop on a Thursday for the first time in months. She hoped he would do some trade, and expected that he wouldn't lie about it. Not that she didn't trust him. She knew he felt guilty about leaving her, but he also always wanted some space. Perhaps they had married too young, or rather, perhaps they hadn't done enough when they *were* young. It wasn't that she wasn't happy, but what if Richard were no longer happy. Her rituals wouldn't be able to control *him*.

After she dropped Holly off at school, an eye on the pavement for any carrier bags, she parked at the car park in the centre of town and did the food shopping for the next couple of days. She preferred not to use larger supermarkets or stock up much in advance, she wanted the freshness of new vegetables and the un-defrosted taste of meat. Poppy was happy in her buggy. It was one where the child faces the parent, all the better to keep a watchful eye.

Of course, being in the centre of town meant she could drop in on Richard at the shop, and she decided to do just that. The bell rang as she entered. Richard was tucked away at the back, embedded amongst the junk, and unfolded himself as he saw her, having been hunched over a blue screen.

"I was going to call you," he said, ebullient. "There's another one of you in Walberswick!"

She sighed. Walberswick was just across the estuary. It was a little too close for comfort.

He continued: "She's in her early fifties, I've been in contact with her this morning, and she's very interested in you."

Julia placed a hand on her forehead. "I'm not sure if I really want this, Richard. Can't we just be left alone?"

He seemed offended. She had to remind herself how interesting he found this research.

"Can't you just pop over for a coffee or something? It'd hardly kill you to be sociable."

She stood silent whilst he retracted the statement, guilt transforming his features like a mask.

"I just worry that you spend too much time with the girls."

She snorted. "They're *my* children, aren't they? Of course I spend time with them."

"Actually, they're *our* children. And you know what I mean. I mean exclusively. You don't go out at all any more. Don't even trust me to look after them in the evening."

"You know we don't know anyone here. And you know what happened last night."

The bell rang over the doorway, and an elderly couple entered. Julia glanced over her shoulder. Now was not the time or place for an argument. She didn't want to argue anyway. She just wanted to be left alone.

Richard scribbled something on a piece of paper and handed it to her. He whispered under his breath, but it felt like a shout. "Just give her a call, ok. It's not going to hurt is it? Just this once, just for me."

She sighed and placed the paper in her pocket. "I'll call when I get home, satisfied?"

She left the shop, not certain that she would.

SEVEN

But then, as it happened, she did.

She knew why. She had never had much contact with any members of her family other than her mother and father. And her father had always seemed distant, he wasn't really part of the family. She had been an only child, no sisters and — as it now appeared impossible due to Richard's research — no brothers. She had grown up in isolation, not distant from other children - she had plenty of friends - but no extended family. Even if this lady was several generations removed, she suddenly felt a tug of kinship. And if she had been right the previous night about the movement of her guardians, might this be the time to contact someone who could have the same responsibilities.

So, it was only an hour or so after she had left Richard that she picked up the phone. And it was only thirty minutes after that when she parked in Ann Carew's driveway.

It wasn't an imposing property. Walberswick could be just as traditional as Southwold, but this was a rundown brick-and-wood building, sandwiched between two other houses that leant vertically against it, as though the property had grown up organically between them, like a misshapen tooth. Despite its look, it was not unwelcoming, yet as she rang the doorbell she had the feeling the owner would be mildly eccentric.

She couldn't have been more mistaken. Ann Carew wasn't much different to herself. A small, brightly dressed woman, with neatly combed hair and a twinkle in her eye. Julia searched her face for some familial resemblance, but nothing obvious connected them, not even a name.

Ann cooed over Poppy as Julia carried her into the hallway. Poppy's eyes grew wide and a smile spread across her face, accentuating her cheeks.

"I have that effect on babies." Ann showed a similar smile herself.

Julia was directed into the sitting room. Immediately she noticed that Ann maintained rituals. The walls were covered in clocks, of various shapes and sizes: round, square, triangular, cuckoo. The timing on each was exact. Each clock also had a full dial, one that delineated the minutes and hours clearly. There were no clocks that displayed the modern obsessions with twelve, three, six and nine. Julia knew that with Ann the time had to be precise.

Ann spoke to her from behind. "A little eccentric, perhaps. But essential, all the same."

Julia wasn't sure what to say. Her mother had impressed she had to keep her rituals secret. She wasn't sure how much Ann might have guessed, but it was blatantly obvious that they shared the same concerns.

"Some tea and biscuits," Ann said, by way of diversion. She moved into the kitchen whilst Julia sat down.

Julia nestled Poppy in the crook of her arm and looked around the room. There was the usual paraphernalia befitting someone of Ann's age: knick-knacks, holiday mementos, photographs. She was unsure if Ann was married, but there were two framed pictures of girls standing beside her. There was no obvious male presence in the room.

Ann returned with two cups, a teapot and a plate of biscuits. Bourbons and shortbread. She glanced over at the photographs. "My daughters, Susan and Kirsty. Susan lives in the States now, and Kirsty in Norfolk. Both of them are doing very well."

Julia nodded. Wondered where *her* daughters would end up, how far from the nest they might fly. She shuddered as she realised they would inevitably distance themselves at some point, but nevertheless her rituals were far-reaching and she could always keep them safe.

"If you're wondering," Ann said, sitting down opposite and pouring out some tea, "I'm divorced. My husband couldn't live with my obsessions any more."

Again, Julia didn't know what to say. She was stirred out of her silence when Ann asked whether she wanted her tea white with sugar, and replied with her preference. She also took two shortbread biscuits from the offered plate, and spoke again once they had each sat back and relaxed.

"My husband doesn't know," she said, in a quiet voice, fearing the world might crack at her words, but needing a release, a shared circumstance to break the awful tension she continuously felt.

"I'm sure he does," Ann replied. "But he probably keeps it quiet. No doubt he worries about you. Hopefully he'll stay with you, but it's not easy, living with people like us."

"Like us?"

"Didn't your mother tell you anything my lovely? We're protecting the world against the Unknown."

"Well, I *am* aware, of course I am."

Ann recognised the defensive tone and changed tack.

"You haven't spoken to anyone about this before, have you?"

Julia squirmed in her seat."I think I better go." She placed her drink on the table next to her, but in her haste the cup slid off the saucer knocking a small plastic clock onto the floor. In a second Ann was kneeling beside her, checking the mechanism. A battery had fallen out of the back. She pushed it in, then picked up at the phone and dialled 123. Julia could hear the voice of the speaking clock sound the correct time, whilst Ann fiddled with the second hand.

When Ann sat down again, Julia noticed her counting under her breath. Ann performed the task in the exact same manner as *she* had been taught. Realisation struck that they were both trapped within the same rituals. Ann's response had been so immediate it couldn't be faked. Her guardians held the same importance as her own.

"I'm sorry," Julia breathed.

"It's ok. Well, now we know where we stand, don't we?"

"Tell me some more about this."

"I'm not sure how much I do know. My mother told me one day I would find a ritual of my own, to take over from her when she died. She was obsessive with cleanliness, would wash plates over and over again until her hands were red raw. From an early age I had an interest in time, and my ritual seemed to come naturally out of that. It was something I gravitated to, rather than something I chose. All I knew was that I didn't want something that would wreck my life in the same way that it had wrecked my mother's."

"What happened?"

"She was in and out of clinics for years. No one understood of course, how could they."

"And your grandparents?"

"I never knew them. Our fate is generation-bound isn't it? We only pass on to our immediate family. I'm sure your situation is the same."

Julia nodded. Then a thought crossed her mind. "How about other family members, do you have any sisters?"

"Only one, but she unfortunately died. No suspicious circumstances. Cancer, I'm afraid."

"And have you tried to contact other relatives?"

Ann shook her head. "It never crossed my mind until recently. Then my daughters bought me a computer and I started looking around, seeing what I could find. There's a lot of hokum about obsessive-compulsive disorders, it's totally misunderstood. On a whim I placed my details on one of those ancestry sites, curiosity

I suppose. I've felt that I've been alone for quite some time now. Perhaps, my lovely, I wanted some answers."

Julia nodded again, waited as Ann poured out more tea. All this tied in with *her* experiences, but it was a dead end wasn't it? Apart from some mutual support, it wouldn't change anything. She didn't need her convictions ratified; everything was clear in her own mind.

Commonly, obsessive-compulsive rituals were characterised as behaviour akin to a mental disorder. She knew this. She also knew that people who 'suffered' were not simply obsessed with doing things repeatedly in a certain way just to satisfy some inner urge, but that they believed they *had* to perform those rituals in order to maintain the safety of loved ones. The research on that was clear. It was a double-edged sword, psychiatrists said, because suggestions of healing them of behaviour simply put their families at risk, this was why it was so hard to 'treat'. However, in Julia's case, and she assumed it was the same with Ann, the psychiatrists' reports had got it all wrong. The reason obsessive-compulsive behaviour was *so* important was *exactly* because it protected their families. Without those rituals she knew her loved ones stability would be rent asunder.

She considered what had happened the previous evening, the certainty she felt that her figurines had been tampered with. Dread teased the base of her neck. Was the situation changing? Could it be that despite her efforts other influences might hold sway? She had to know whether Ann had experienced a similar feeling. What if everything were to escalate? Maybe safety would be found in numbers.

"I'm not sure what I'm looking for," she began. "It's Richard who is obsessed with ancestry, and having exhausted his own line he's decided to try mine. But now that I'm here perhaps I should ask you a question. Have you noticed any differences recently, anything happening which is genuinely out of the ordinary?"

Ann sat forwards. "I think it's no coincidence that you're here at this time," she said. "Something seems to be changing, I can't quite put my finger on it, but I'm older than you and I can sense something isn't quite right. I've no physical proof, just a tingling sensation in my spine. And don't laugh that off, I've had such suspicions before."

"What can we do?"

"Wait? What else can we do?"

"Wait for what?"

"Just wait for something to happen."

EIGHT

Julia returned to their Southwold home in trepidation, feeling more than a little disorganised. Her years of rituals hadn't prepared her for this. Ann had intimated that something could threaten them way beyond the safety that their guardians could provide. It was the Unknown that frightened her, which played upon the security of her children.

She quickly fed Poppy, a little faster than she would normally have done but time was getting away and she had to collect Holly from school. Setting out again her hands gripped the steering wheel in frustration as she realised she would be cutting it fine to arrive before the bell. She performed her counting rituals under her breath. What with the traffic, and Poppy crying in her carrycot — possibly due to indigestion — and the fear of not collecting

Holly on time, a pressure began to build within her head which the rituals could only just keep at bay.

It was a nightmare parking at the school at the best of times, although she found a place opposite the entrance on the other side of the road. Children were spilling out through the doors, collected by parents with smiles on their faces. She could see Holly jogging for position at the back. Fear ripped through her as Holly recognised their car. Julia was torn between leaving Poppy in her carrycot and heading across the road, or waiting for Holly to cross by herself. Both options horrified her, and she swore under her breath at Richard whose investigations had disrupted her routine.

Storming out of the vehicle she shouted for Holly to remain still. She was aware of some hysteria in her voice. Several of the parents turned to look her way. Julia knew it wasn't a busy road, not a single car had passed since she parked, but that wasn't the point. Vehicles could come at any time, particularly at this time of day. Thankfully Holly heard her and didn't move. Julia unbuckled the carry cot and traversed the road, collected Holly, and then safely made the journey back again.

"Mum, can Chloe come over this afternoon?" Holly gripped her hand tightly. "*Please?*"

Julia shook her head. "Not today."

"But I never have anyone over."

"I'm just going to be too busy darling."

Julia opened the car door for Holly, played the touching-the-roof game, which had now become permanent, and then secured Poppy's carrycot once again.

Setting off she noticed some of the other mothers tilt their heads. She knew they were talking about her. It wasn't easy to make friends here, and she increasingly didn't want to. There were too many variables, too many challenges involved in inviting someone into their house, particularly a child. What if her guardians were disrupted, knocked into? Poppy would be playmate sufficient for Holly once she got older. In the back of her mind, she knew that was the reason they had conceived a second child.

Once home she put Poppy down for another nap. Holly busied herself with a few of her dolls, and after quickly checking her figurines Julia played with her for the remainder of the afternoon. Before she knew it, she was cooking and Richard was home. He appeared excited, and she asked him immediately about his meeting with Ann.

"Well, she was pleasant enough. I felt comfortable with her. Although I don't suppose we'll need to meet again any time soon."

She watched as his expression lost a little of the excitement. What was he expecting? A family reunion?

"Nothing else? No photographs, no other information?"

She sighed. "You know I'm not really into all this Richard, I have enough to think about as it is."

"Well, forgive me if I was hoping for something more."

She expected him to sulk, enter the living room and switch on his computer for more pointless research, but instead he stood watching as she diced carrots.

"It's been a quiet day at work," he said. "I was able to do some more research. Hopefully I've found something that you might actually find interesting."

She tipped the carrots into the saucepan, and began topping and tailing some sprouts to go with them. "Tell away."

"I think I've managed to trace you back to 1154. To a place called Woolpit, commonly derived from Wolf Pit, near Bury St Edmunds. As you know, that's only about ninety minutes from here."

"We went to Bury once, didn't we?" she said, remembering flint and stone city walls, an expanse of green, a lively market.

"Yep, shortly after we moved here. Anyway, here's where it gets really interesting. There's a legend surrounding your family."

She laughed. "A legend?" But her laugh felt hollow, even to herself. Did she really need to hear this?

"Exactly! Listen to this. Apparently two children were found wandering in the Woolpit area who claimed to have come from *inside* the Earth. Their skin was green, they could eat only beans, and eventually the boy died. The girl, however, went on to marry a local man after having worked for a while within the house of a Richard de Calne. Some records state they had no children, but I managed to delve a little deeper by — well, to be honest, I closed up the shop this afternoon and drove over there — looking into the local parish records. I'm not one hundred percent certain, but it does seem that a girl was born to this Agnes lady, as she was subsequently called, and *that* girl's ancestry leads all the way up to you."

Julia bundled several potatoes out of a polythene bag and into the sink, rubbing their surfaces to release the dirt, before picking them out individually and peeling them.

"Green children?"

"They're even depicted on the village sign. Of course, there are many variations of the tale, and the greenness appears to be related to diet. The children initially seemed unable to speak English, but after a while the girl learnt it. She explained they had come from a place called St Martin's Land, which had its own sun. It wasn't as powerful as ours, their world seemed to be in perpetual twilight. Anyway, as I was saying, once they began to eat properly they lost the greenish tint to their skin. Of course, they didn't really come out of the ground," he laughed, "but there is no evidence to say how they got there. Somehow malnourished, the girl regained enough strength to get back into regular society. The boy, as I said, died."

Richard's words washed over her from the moment he mentioned St Martin's Land. Julia dropped the potato peeler into the sink, she felt her legs grow weak, and a radiance that seemed to be emanating within her head clouded her vision in a honeyed glow. Suddenly, she gasped and almost fell, as though she had ascended and found her footing, or had expected another step at the top of the stairs to find one wasn't there.

She was aware of Richard holding her. Her forehead was wet, she wondered if she had been about to faint. She'd experienced something similar when pregnant with Holly, but that was understandable under the circumstances. Now she felt like a fool.

"Are you ok?"

"Yes. Yes, I think so. Just got a bit dizzy, that's all."

But it wasn't all, and she knew it. The mention of St Martin's Land had hit her like a brick. She didn't know what it was, but she knew she had to protect it. At all costs.

RICHARD

ONE

Richard hadn't known what to expect before he told Julia about the green children, other than she might laugh it off, greet it with her usual indifference, or suggest that he had got it wrong and they were nothing to do with her. But whilst he was convinced she *hadn't* heard of them before, her reaction had taken him by surprise. After she almost fainted, she refused to discuss it with him further. She had actually suggested he leave the kitchen whilst she finished preparing dinner, and hardly spoke to him at all until they got ready for bed later that night. When he did try to raise the subject matter just as he drifted to sleep, her reply was short and sharp: 'drop it'.

But he didn't sleep. And neither did she. At around one in the morning he heard her get up and spend some time downstairs. He knew it wasn't an irregular occurrence, Julia had had sleepless nights since the death of her mother, and he assumed she caught up with her sleep during the day when Holly was at school. He rarely went downstairs to see how she was, having got blasted for it several years ago. Sometimes, it seemed, she needed some quiet time.

So, instead of getting up, he just lay there. Drifting in and out of consciousness, reflecting on the information he had found, not all of which he had managed to mention to Julia before she shut him out. On the peripheries of sleep he felt he were reliving the previous day, it came to him complete, replayed, as real as when it happened.

The breakthrough had come that morning. As usual he had driven to work, manoeuvring his Renault Megane through the narrow Southwold streets. Although it had been early, pedestrians meandered from path to road, old age almost a form of drunkenness. This displacement might have kept them unstable with the conviction of being young, in much the same way as drunks believe they are sober, or at least, capable. Richard cursed them.

He drummed his fingers against the steering wheel as a couple, hand in hand, paused in the middle of the road. Once they'd decided their direction, he was able to turn into the narrow pathway that led to the back of the shop. The car bleated electronically as he locked the doors and Richard shook his head. He would have to get that fixed.

He turned on the light as he entered the antiques shop, but the place remained dingy. Cobwebs hung half-heartedly from the upper reaches, the dark propping them in place. The air was thin. They might have been at high altitude rather than the flatness of the Suffolk coast, but it was dust that gave the impression of breathlessness.

It was a little early to open up. He still wasn't used to the way things were done in this town. It was a throwback to older, not always better, times.

Regardless of that, he loved it here.

Squeezing past the junk into the back room he fetched the cashbox that he kept in the drawer of a Georgian writing desk. That desk should have been sold long ago, but he didn't like to part with it. Its presence gave his office the appearance of a home.

He removed the float and re-entered the main area of the shop, opening the till. It rang hollow, almost unloved. The plastic drawer had breadcrumbs stuck in the corners, remnants of many a sandwich eaten during sales. He'd once tried to remove them, taking out the drawer and shaking it vigorously, but not only did they stick fast but he'd had a devil of a job replacing it afterwards. Since then he lived with the crumbs.

He cast his eye around the shop. The antiques themselves were next to spotless. It was the peripheries - the hidden places - that the dust and grime preferred, the shop collected the detritus of his thoughts. Not that those thoughts were dark — although there were some things he wouldn't want to reveal to Julia. It was more a case of whilst he was here, he could be himself.

Julia rarely visited him at work, so that morning had been the exception. There was Poppy to look after, as if she'd taken over in a relay race after Holly had started school. Even without the children Richard was sure Julia would be kept busy at home. Their house was always spotless.

It hadn't been clear from the start of their courtship — or indeed, their marriage — but gradually she had become a caricature of a housewife. A thick straw mat stood outside both their front and back doors. Shoes had to be wiped and taken off before entering. Slippers on immediately. If he ran his finger along the mantelpiece no dirty residue would blemish his skin. Not that he did so, except on those occasions when he wanted to prove to her that the house was clean.

Their objects and object d'art were arranged precisely. Even Holly and Poppy's toys were collected in ordered piles in plastic containers. Although she was at home all day, Richard still didn't know where Julia found the time.

He was sure it hadn't always been like that, yet memories blurred to the extent that he couldn't be positive. He was thirty-eight, Julia thirty-three. They had been married eight years. Certainly no more than that. He hadn't got into the antiques business until after they had moved to Southwold. It was an early retirement location. A *bloody* early retirement. Already there was a certain stiffness permeating his bones. It wouldn't be long before they found it impossible to leave.

Whilst that was fanciful, he did consider whether being surrounded by the belongings of the dead, by furniture and trinkets of times past, prematurely aged him. Perhaps it wouldn't be long before he wore a pale brown cardigan and smoked a pipe in the back room, flicking through old newspapers, and occasionally breaking off a piece of Caley's traditional chocolate. Only a pint of Adnams at lunchtime might save him.

He allowed himself a smile. It wasn't quite that bad. He checked his watch again, saw there were ten minutes before opening. Squeezing through the junk into the back room he turned on his computer. There was just time to check his emails, to see whether any of his genealogy trails had borne fruit.

Richard's family history had long been documented. Rather selfishly, he thought, an uncle of his who wasn't even related by blood had researched the line of Dean's back to Elizabethan times. Just as Richard developed an interest in the family, he was presented with that fait accompli. Poppy's birth had spurred him. A second daughter to kill off the family name, rather than a son who would carry it on. Piqued by his uncle's intrusions, Richard decided to research his wife's genealogical origins. There was a certain sense of retribution to be had. Even honour.

So he was pleased to see an email from Ann Carew sent via the Genes Reunited website, especially so because she lived close to them. If only he could persuade Julia to visit, then perhaps he could continue with his research on a face-to-face basis, rather than relying on the pc. Leaving his computer on, he returned to the front of the shop, and sliding the deadbolts he unlocked the door. A faint mist entered, like the ghosts of those who had died insisting on cohabiting with their furniture. The sun would soon clear that up. They were on the cusp of summer. An almost-June day. It wouldn't be long before the tourists descended and he could inflate his prices again. Let the good times roll.

But the shop was quiet that morning, like most mornings. Richard sat at the computer in the back room, his ear open for the bell. Pushed to the back of his mind went his wonderings as to what Julia did whilst he was asleep, most of which he accounted for as the strange sleep patterns engendered when young children were in the house. He knew that he'd find time spent with them during the day to be exhausting, and whilst he loved them that was partly why he had opened the shop. To get some peace and quiet.

Julia's maiden name had been Barras, adapted from the Saxon word, *Baerwas*, meaning a place amongst trees. Or in some accounts, the dweller who lived outside the fortress. Both of which, he surmised, more or less meant the same thing. The Internet had revealed over two million references to that name online, although obviously most were completely unconnected with Julia, and only by painstakingly backtracking through the records had he managed to trace any links. Of course, his problem was made all the more difficult as he had never traced any male heirs, so her maiden name became incidental when tracing her female line. With each generation, the surname proved a dead end and ultimately the trail had dried up completely.

Not surprising considering the timeline, but if anything this provoked Richard's tenacity.

Julia was an attractive woman, and it certainly seemed she had passed the beauty genes onto her daughters. Good cheekbones, delicate nose, kissable mouth. Breeding stock if ever he saw it. Not that Richard had married her with that in mind, far from it. The children had been her idea. Not his.

Most of Julia's family were dead. Her parents had birthed her at a late age, and her father had died before Richard had known her. Her mother had followed within a few years. Neither of them had contracted any horrible diseases, but simply passed away in their sleep. Julia had no siblings, and whilst he had located other living relatives he had so far refrained from suggesting that they contact them.

Generally, this was because Julia was more or less ambivalent to his findings. Often she would simply shrug and suggest that he spent less time at the computer. On better days she would take a look, but for her the past was simply full of dead people and not worthy of examination. She seemed to have no interest in her lineage from a historical point of view, whereas Richard felt imbued by the sense of travelling through time — stuck in fast forward — whereby history was the only means of looking back.

Often he wondered whether her dead parents made retrospection difficult. Both of his were still alive. He had read somewhere that it is only when a parent dies that the offspring becomes truly aware of mortality. To a degree, he subscribed to that theory, yet believed it also came into play when a child was born. The miracle of life simply acknowledged the other side of the coin. The depressing reality of death.

Richard wondered whether his future ancestors might

eventually trace him. Come to visit the spot at which Dean's Antiques once sat, in a Southwold in a dystopian future dominated by some garish theme park. That is, if its fate was not to disappear under the sea.

Just along the coast from Southwold was the small town of Dunwich, which to a large extent had succumbed to the sea in the early 1900's. Until the 1950s, it was still easy to find identifiable lumps of masonry on the beach, and as late as 1985, the bones of those buried in All Saints' graveyard protruded gruesomely from the cliff, and a single gravestone, to John Brinkley Easey, stood in an inconceivably bleak loneliness at the cliff top.

Richard didn't quite live in the past, but often he thought he was more comfortable with it.

The birth of Holly and then Poppy had, in some ways, confused him. It confirmed that he was simply part of life's spiral, undermined his importance in the same stroke that it emphasised it. If anything, the births had pushed him even further into the past. Nudged him into a corner. The future history of his daughters threatened to sweep him aside.

Yet the past was rich, wasn't it? Just as valuable and valid as the future. Not only that but it had actually existed, whereas at some point the future might never be. Although of course, Richard acknowledged, if the future never was then the fact that history had once been would no longer be relevant. He sighed. It was on days like these that he wondered just what he was doing with his life.

It was then that Julia entered the shop with Poppy, and he had given her the information about Ann. *And* had managed — he hoped — to persuade her to visit. After she left he realised that he wanted to impress her, that more than anything else he needed to please her, to be accepted by her. It seemed a strange thing to need from a wife, surely that should be a given, but for some reason of late he had found her dismissive, and he felt the only way he could prove himself was through the research.

After Julia left, the bell rang again. He watched the potential purchaser from the back room, wary of appearing to pounce on a sale. Better to be nonchalant and let the customer come to him, for them to decide in their minds how much they might pay for an item, before he forced a price onto them which they might well reject.

Shopkeeping was about balance, walking the tightrope of approachability. Speak to some customers too soon and they flee with a fake smile on their faces, yet others would be happy to chat for an hour about the weather and their families and pick up a piece at the end of it almost as an afterthought. And knowing which type of customer was which was exactly what Richard was good at. The person who entered the shop now wouldn't buy anything, he knew that. They were too young and probably wouldn't stay for longer than a quick scan of his stock.

Richard turned his attention to the computer, just as a new message popped in his inbox. The sender's name was Susanne Lee and was new to him. This wasn't particularly surprising as many of the genealogy websites he visited had a function for leaving contact details when searching for a particular lineage, and whilst most of the contacts Richard had received from those links were usually those asking for information rather than providing it, inevitably the name association kicked up at least something that he might count or discount. If only Julia held more of an interest, then his time spent at the machine might be worth it.

He clicked open the message. After some preliminary

introductions there seemed to be some worth in the email. A branch of the family that had split into three ways a couple of hundred years ago had proved elusive when tracing the third daughter that had been born. Indications were that she hadn't married, although Richard could find no records to suggest she died a spinster.

Now it was suggested that she *had* indeed married, and had borne a daughter. That line had continued to the present day, and the woman emailing him might well be related to Julia. An incredibly distant cousin, several times removed, could open up many new lines of enquiry that would be exciting to pursue for a while. Similarities were apparent even in the writing style: numerous exclamation marks and smiley faces of the sort that Julia used to send him when they first got together. Then he smiled. Surely that was indicative of females everywhere...

He looked up as the youth left the shop, then rose and made sure that nothing had left without being paid for. Southwold wasn't that kind of town, but you could never be too sure. Having satisfied himself that even the dust hadn't been disturbed, Richard returned to the computer and answered the email with a brief acknowledgement and the promise of following up the line of enquiry later.

It was only later, however, that he examined that information in depth and realised the new family line went as far back as 1154. And then he had closed the shop and made the journey to Woolpit to search through church records.

It was as he had told Julia, the so-called Green children, aged approximately five and eight, had been found wandering in the wolf pit at Woolpit in Suffolk. They seemed disorientated, didn't speak English, and initially refused any food they were given except for green beans, which they devoured hungrily. After a short while the boy had died, but the girl went into service for local landowner Richard de Calne and had subsequently married.

Online reports had suggested no children, but Richard was fairly certain that hadn't been the case. Most people were childbearing in those days, and unless there were any physical problems then it seemed unlikely for her to be barren. Although he had made a leap of faith for the final connection, a child bearing the same surname had showed in later records, and the pull of history had drawn him towards her.

There had been no indication that local folk had subsequently looked for the entrance to St Martin's Land, as the girl had described it, something that Richard had found infuriating, but then records weren't records as such, only legends as he had informed Julia. In any event, if she was traced as far back as that girl, then there was no indication he could go back further.

Unless he descended into the bowels of the earth itself.

TWO

He awoke the next morning from a disturbing dream. He recognised the source: it was meshed together from the 1960 movie version of H.G. Wells' *The Time Machine* and from his own childhood. He had a memory of being buried in the sand on some nameless beach, his father laughing as it was packed down around him. There was a frisson of fear as he realised he couldn't move, yet it was tempered by the knowledge that his father would be able to save him before the tide came in. In the memory, of course, this is exactly what had happened, although for a long time that tenacious edge of being trapped had haunted him. At that age — eight, possibly — the tightrope of life and death was suddenly presented to him, and that sense of dread had permeated all through his life.

In the dream however, as his father slapped the spade down on the last patch of crinkly sand, he could feel a shift in the substance beneath him. As though he were in a giant egg timer, the sand was funnelling away beneath his feet, the air created in the gap sucking him down, away from his father, away from the brightness of the blue sky, away from all that he had known.

As he fell within the earth, the circle of light where his head had been became smaller and smaller, his father's face leaning over into the hole, eclipsing the view, until all that existed was blackness.

He dream-fell. Darkness rushed around him in a whisper, but he had the feeling that if he tried to stand he would be able to do so. So he *forced* himself to stop, and discovered he was already on the ground. Three separate tunnels were before him, each as black as each other. He looked up, but there was not even the pinprick of light. In his waking state he wondered how he could see at all, but in the dream he hadn't considered it. He only had to choose between the tunnels.

Reaching into his pocket he pulled out a coin. Heads, left. Tails, right. On its side, middle. Flicking it into the air it disappeared, then a chink of metal on the ground told him it had landed. When he looked, the coin was on its side.

He took the middle route. As he progressed, lighted torches began to illuminate the way. He could see flickering shadows that were definitely people, dotted on ledges high above. Suddenly he realised he was no longer his eight-year old self, but his current self. He reached up and collected one of the burning torches, carried it before him, its light-shadow distorting his view as it left retina burns back-dropped against the dark.

Mumbles resonated around him, language unintelligible. He entered a larger chamber, much better lit, a circular stage where hairy faces and semi-naked bodies held court. Hands gripped his shoulders from behind and he was thrust into the centre. He recognised the figures as the Morlock, the underground descendents of Wells' novel who enslaved the lives of the Eloi who lived above ground.

That was the crux of the novel as he remembered it. The seemingly Neanderthal genetic line actually holding sway over the more poetic lifestyle of those above. The failure of good to triumph over evil, or perhaps less dramatically, the failure of innocence to triumph over brutality. Not a concept restricted to underground/overground, of course. There were plenty of political parallels that could be drawn.

Not that this came to him in the dream. He had been tripped, pushed to the floor with his face full of dirt, the flaming torch forced from his grip, flaying away from him. As he watched it, the fire sputtered, burning ashes scattered outwards like discharged fireworks, before it came to rest too far away to be used as a weapon.

It was then that he had awoken. Julia was beside him in bed, but her body was cool. He had the feeling that she had just returned from a nightly wander. Glancing over at the clock he only had time to register it was 3:34am before falling back to a dreamless sleep.

The following day the shop was mildly busy, he sold a few choice items — enough to cover the cost of opening for the week. It wasn't that they needed the shop for income, but he had to justify its existence, and who knew, in the future when their funds were depleted he might need to have something for their lifestyle to tick over.

He still had time for research, but it was half-hearted. Stalling at the legend he had reached the end of the road, and researching the legend itself proved just as fruitless. There was no more information to be found than he had already unearthed. A copycat case had been reported in Spain, a few hundred years after the 'original', but that was easily dismissed because the details were more or less identical, not simply a similar incident. Instead, he thought laterally, decided to research other 'dwellers' within the Earth. Not that he considered for a moment the veracity of the green story. The children's colour, even if it were green, was no doubt down to diet. Having read around the topic it didn't seem unusual for children to be abandoned in those times — tired, malnourished, it was lucky they had survived at all. If it wasn't for the green tint to their skin there wouldn't have been any legend.

However, knowing all this didn't dampen his enthusiasm. Now that a few contacts had been made he was already considering a reunion party, something that Julia would have to embrace and which he was sure would do her good. She hadn't seemed averse to meeting Ann, and whilst he couldn't understand her 'funny turn' the previous evening, he couldn't believe she would be totally against it. Not only that, but he knew she was withdrawing into herself, particularly since Poppy's birth, and that concerned him. Not to the extent that he would involve a GP, but enough to think of ways around the situation.

And she had been off with him too, dismissive, sarcastic sometimes. That wasn't any way to live in a marriage.

So, to while away a few hours, he read through several other legends associated with what he found was commonly called Hollow Earth. Several cultures' stories — such as the Hindu legend of Patal Lok, or the Chinese city Hsi Tien - seemed to suggest that the earth was hollow. That another land existed within, with a paler sun, often with an entrance point around one of the Poles. Richard snorted at the possibility. He held the same beliefs when faced with UFOs or other unexplained behaviour. If these people did exist, then why should they hide themselves away? Surely there would be more than a few urban legends and bits and pieces on the Internet. Unless it was all hushed up, which he found equally difficult to believe.

And of course, even within these legends there was no commonality of substance. The underground dwellers ranged from super-intelligent beings originally from outer space whose technologies far outstripped our own, to subhuman demons crawling their way up the evolutionary ladder with an eye on the 'real' world as their prize.

It was all too nonsensical for him.

There were those who did take it seriously however. He discovered a website for a team intending to fund an expedition to the North Pole, with a view to discovering the entrance to Hollow Earth. On the face of it, it looked legitimate, with backing from a Dutch financier, Wilhelm Hagen. Yet it didn't ring true to Richard. Essentially they were asking for public funding to make the journey, to take a 'select' number of 'tourists' with them. It seemed more like a blatant cockamamie scam as he read through the information, backed with pseudo-scientific nonsense and unsubstantiated claims.

It wasn't that there was little information to back up the expedition, more that there was too much of it. An elaborate hoax would need an elaborate background in order to make it sound authentic, whereas if all the information before him was genuine then — as he considered earlier — it would surely be common public knowledge. As usual, conspiracy theories abounded.

Just for fun, though, and maybe a nagging interest, he signed up for their newsletter and progress reports. It would give him something to read during the quiet hours if nothing else.

THREE

When he returned home from work that evening Julia had already prepared a meal. Of late, their mealtimes had been shunted into the middle of the evening, and whilst she didn't say anything he took it as a peace offering from their semi-argument of the previous night. Once Holly and Poppy were asleep they snuggled up on the sofa, arms and legs entwined, with something on the television that neither of them were interested in but which they were happy to watch together.

He was reminded of the early days of their courtship and marriage. Doing the 'nothing' things which were so important simply because they were shared. Where the slightest nod, sigh, or the way Julia did the washing up — a multitude of nuances —

imbued him with a warmness of appreciation that made him love her all the more.

In his previous job, a cynic had once told him that 'love fades'. He had snorted derisory at the time, unable to comprehend the concept. But even if he didn't agree with it now, he knew that love became tempered, rationalised, set in routine. It didn't go, but became ghostly, ethereal, not quite as important as other things.

Without a doubt, he realised Julia knew that too. And it was their children that had taken this away from them, diverted, subverted, their feelings. There just wasn't enough love to go around.

"What have you been up to today?"

She snuggled closer. "Not much. I've been sleeping. I feel worn out."

"Maybe you've got a cold."

"Maybe."

"I've been doing more research, want to hear about it?"

"Not sure."

"It's interesting."

"Sure it is, Sherlock."

"Are you going to contact Ann again?"

Julia's brow furrowed. He could feel it under his fingertips as he had been lightly stroking the top of her head.

"I think I will."

"Good."

"Tell me more about this St Martin's Land."

Richard didn't have much more to tell her than he had the previous evening. Again he reiterated how far he had managed to trace back her family, how one pivotal contact had opened up a new line of investigation, and how it certainly seemed possible she had been descended from the girl who came out of the Earth.

"That's nonsense, isn't it?"

"Well, that she came out of the earth, yes. The fact that she was found wandering with her brother, less so."

"Interesting there was a brother, don't you think?"

He nodded. "Haven't found another male line so far."

"I can't quite believe this, you know. The way that our lives can trail so far back into the past. I've been a bit of a bitch about it, I know."

"I wouldn't go that far."

"Perhaps you should."

They were silent for a while. The programme ended and a reality police show started. Richard reached for the remote and turned it off.

Julia placed her hand on his chest. "This St Martin's Land. When you mentioned it, I knew of it."

"You *knew* of it?"

"Well, not in detail. But it resonated within me. Deeply." She placed a hand on her heart. "Frankly, it worried me."

Richard was tempted to laugh it off, to play it down, but her voice was too intense.

"There's something else," she said. "There is a connection between me and Ann, something we share, something that binds us. It's not just a family thing, we're completely different in that respect. But it's more, and I'm only just feeling that I'm grasping the edge of it."

"Sounds like you're talking in riddles to me."

"Maybe I can't describe it any other way."

She turned her face towards his and he was shocked to notice that her eyes were wet, as though viewed under water.

"Oh babe!"

She smiled, then. "Am I really still a babe at my age?"

"You'll always be my babe."

"Sounds weird coming out of your mouth now."

He shrugged. "We're not as old as we think we are."

Julia dried her eyes before she spoke again.

"Don't laugh at me, Richard, but I'm frightened."

"Frightened? Frightened of what?"

"I don't know. You, me, our children. Our safety. I thought I had it all worked out, but now I'm not so sure."

"Riddles again."

"Yes, maybe. Hold me."

"I am holding you."

"Tighter."

He squeezed her as hard as he could.

"Maybe I need some family around me so I don't feel quite so alone."

"Other than me?"

"Yes, other than you. Not that you're not enough, but, you know."

"You're actually open to me contacting more family members?"

"Yes."

He smiled. "Good. Looks like all my hard work wasn't for nothing after all."

They exchanged a few affectionate kisses, then Julia decided to check on the children before getting ready for bed. He watched her ascend the stairs, then turned on his computer for the first time that evening. Collating as many email addresses as he could, he fanned out invitations across the net, to all corners of the earth. Considering he had been researching for over a year it wasn't surprising when some of them bounced back as unavailable, but there was more than enough there to keep Julia going.

He briefly wondered about her fears, but attributed them to a lack of belonging. Hopefully, his endeavours would change that.

Amongst his emails were also seven updates on the Hollow Earth expedition. It seemed as a new recruit he had been sent all the information reports they had previously cascaded to their followers. There was even a 'personal' message from Wilhelm Hagen himself.

Richard scanned a couple of them. According to the organisers, Eskimos believed there was a hole in the Arctic Ocean. And mirages of land observed by several Arctic explorers indicated that the most plausible location for a north polar opening was located at 84.4 N latitude, 141 E longitude. These figures meant nothing to him, although having specifics lent believability to what he was reading.

Independent reports suggested that land had been sighted over the Arctic wastes by different explorers from different directions at different times, and always seen in the same location, whether from Greenland, Alaska or northern Russia. The Russians called it Sannikov land, and had seen it north of the New Siberian Islands. Admiral Peary, on his way to the pole in 1909, sighted land northwest of Cape Thomas Hubbard on the northwest coast of Ellesmere Island in Northern Canada. With him, Lt. Green, MacMillan, and their Eskimos also saw it - and even later went on an expedition to find it, only turning back when their Eskimos claimed it to be mist. Admiral Peary named it Crocker land. Dr. Cook on his way to the pole in 1906 saw it also towards the northwest of his trek from Ellesmere Island. Then from Harrison

Bay on the north coast of Alaska, Captain Keenan sighted land also towards the northwest.

The emails continued that Jan Lamprecht in his book, *Hollow Planets*, made an excellent case that these sightings of mirages of land in the arctic, could actually be land within a polar opening, seen as a doubly inverted mirage caused by the warm air that comes up from the polar hole.

The polar expedition proposed that the hidden land within the north polar region be located. The email also proposed that the land is inhabited. Richard paused to read the story of the Scandinavian explorer Olaf Jansen and his father who entered through the north polar opening in 1829. Their account maintained the people were friendly, highly advanced in the sciences, arts, and geometry. And that they were ardent worshipers of the Israelite god Jehovah, whom they believed had a throne on the sun of inner earth.

Richard continued to read, not without some amusement, that it was speculated their God was Jehovah. That these peoples of inner earth were actually the legendary Lost Ten Tribes of Israel, whom, the Apocryphal author Esdras wrote, escaped the Assyrians in 687 BC and migrated to a region in the north called Arsareth. This land, with its gold, abundance of precious stones, metals and giant forests, was claimed as a veritable Garden of Eden. Indeed, Olaf Jansen considered that this is where the original Garden of Eden is located - within Hollow Earth. His account states he was taken there on a monorail by friendly inner earth inhabitants, and reported that on the highest mountain plateau of the inner continent the Garden of Eden exists where "...all manner of fruits, vines, shrubs, trees, and flowers grow in riotous profusion. In this garden four rivers have their source in a mighty artesian fountain. They divide and flow in four directions. The place is called by the inhabitants, the 'navel of the earth' or the beginning, 'the cradle of the human race.' The names of the rivers are Euphrates, the Pison, the Gihon, and the Hiddekel."

Armed with this information the Hollow Earth expedition postulated that a revolutionary change was required in all areas of history, education, the sciences and art. That the theory of gravity would need to be revised to account for an inner earth surface upon which people could dwell normal earth-bound lives with their feet firmly planted on the ground, and not floating around in zero gravity, as orthodox science maintained would be the case. The theory of evolution would be dealt a decisive blow with the establishment of the location of the actual, original Garden of Eden, indicating the historical accuracy of the Bible and the reality of Adam and Eve.

Finally, in supposed extracts from the Lost Books of the Bible, Richard read that Adam and Eve originated from inner earth. After being driven from the Garden of Eden by God for partaking of the forbidden fruit, they were told to dwell in the Cave of Treasures, where they got lost. When they finally found their way out, the sun that came up in the morning was different than the soft sunlight in Eden. This new sun burned them. The hotter, harsher sun that shines on the outside of our world, was different from the sun that shines in the Garden of Eden.

Richard stopped reading. There was no doubt in his mind that these guys were lunatics. At the end of each email there was information about signing up for the expedition, a trip where they were looking for investments of several million pounds to charter a Russian nuclear icebreaker, although, of course, no guarantees could be made that the opening to inner Earth might be found. He considered it was a trip for rich people with too much money and too much time on their hands. Nevertheless, the similarities between the described land and those that had been reported in relation to the Green children were intriguing, even if those entrances were several thousand miles apart.

On impulse, he shot an email back mentioning Julia and her green credentials. Even as he did so he wondered why he'd been so impetuous, but it was too late to stop and he supposed they would take no notice. It wasn't as if they really believed this stuff, did they? Surely it was little more than a scam.

FOUR

He stayed up awhile longer, reading the progress reports about the expedition which seemed to constantly stall. The excuse was lack of funds although there was some indication of other forces at work. Nothing specific, but maybe gremlins in the machine creating confusion and delays. No doubt there was a conspiracy theory surrounding that, rather than the incompetence of the organisers themselves.

Before he knew it, a couple of hours had passed. It was almost midnight and he realised with some horror that Julia had long gone to bed. His computer was a time-eating machine, and he should have followed her ages ago, especially since she had intimated they might make love.

He turned off the pc, yawned, then stood up and shook his legs to get some movement back. Heading over towards the lamp illuminating the room, he clicked the switch and plunged himself into darkness.

There was a sound, like glass sliding on metal. Quite faint, but purposeful. Immediately he switched on the light and looked around. Nothing obvious was making the noise. He turned off the light once more, but the noise came again. He wondered if it was something to do with the bulb, an expenditure of electricity rattling around inside it. Turning on the light it stopped for a third time.

He walked to the foot of the stairs, and turned on the hall light before returning to the living room and switching off the lamp again. Heading back to the hallway he stood and listened, the light casting a glow that permeated into the other room. He heard the noise again, and something caught his eye.

An object was moving in the cabinet containing Julia's figurines. One of the Laliques caught the light from the doorway, and almost imperceptibly it was refracted across the room, rainbowing along the walls as it turned. Richard caught his breath. Was something trapped behind there? They had a minor problem with mice when they first obtained the property, although he couldn't see how it could have entered the cabinet. As far as he knew the door was secure, it was somewhat off bounds even to himself.

It wasn't easy to discern in the half-light, and he was reluctant to throw the main switch, but it appeared two of the figures were changing places with a deliberate movement. Of course, this couldn't be so, it had to be a trick of the light, but nevertheless it fascinated him and transfixed his gaze, which meant he jumped all the more when Julia placed a hand on his shoulder.

"Jesus!"

"What is it?" she whispered.

"Something's happening in your cabinet."

Her fingers dug into his shoulder, and he felt the surface skin tear.

"Probably nothing," he added. Not convinced.

"Keep looking."

They watched cheek to cheek, their breath intermingling, Richard detecting the smell of toothpaste. Suddenly there was a crash and the cabinet door swung open. Julia hit the main light and raced into the room, desperation etched over her features. Her figurines were inexplicably scattered across the carpet, thankfully intact. Richard could hear her counting manically under her breath as she collected them swiftly, edging on her knees towards the cabinet in an attempt to replace them.

He glanced into its interior, but there was nothing to suggest any movement. Whatever had caused it had gone.

But suddenly there was a noise above their heads. A thump sounding like someone had fallen out of bed. Julia turned her terrified gaze towards him, her face streaked with tears, her eyes wild in fright. Seemingly immobile she held her head in her hands, which was how Richard saw her as he raced up the stairs.

He tried to take them two at a time, but faltered and fell. A scrabbling sound came from the children's bedroom, insectoid in nature. His heart pounded as he flung open the door that was usually ajar.

What did he see? An open window, an empty bed, Poppy crying in her cot. And out of the window, as he reached it breathless, two squat figures pulling Holly along between them, racing at unnatural speeds until they hit the horizon where fields met sky, and disappeared.

WILHELM

ONE

Wilhelm clicked open his emails. He always handled this particular account, and whilst his secretary was more than aware of his Hollow Earth interests, he wanted to keep incoming information secret. Either because he considered it classified until he released it, or because there were enough nut-jobs willing to discredit him that he didn't want their influence rubbing off on her.

He wasn't getting any younger, but keeping his stature was paramount. Born in 1944, he had reached the age where he could no longer convince himself that he had avoided the ageing process, even if the ravages of time had held off for a considerable number of years. And despite his great wealth, estimated by *Forbes* at two billion pounds, no amount of potential plastic surgery was going to save him from the grave. For a man such as him, with his expectations and desires, it was almost tantamount to treason.

He ran a hand through his hair which had recently started to grey. The skin on his fingers was becoming wrinkled, almost waxy. He needed eye drops when he awoke in the morning, and was on tablets due to high blood pressure. He wasn't so much falling apart as falling inwards. It pained him.

Wilhelm August Hagen had begun his career as a trainee in a Norwegian shipbrokering company, and through hard work and determination now owned over fifty oil tankers, held major interests in oil rigs and fish farming, and had a sideline in expensive but selectively profitable cruise ships to Antarctica. It was in that latter field that he had come to hear of the theories of Hollow Earth, and the possibility of an entrance through the opposite pole.

The subject had fascinated him from the start, then gradually become an obsession. And like most of his obsessions, he had to follow it through. Despite his wealth, however, he didn't want to barge in. There was plenty of money to be lost following that route, and whilst he wasn't particularly cautious in his business dealings he also wasn't an idiot. Fund an expensive trip to try and find something and fail? No, it was beneath him. Much better to start a campaign to willingly get scientists on board — to use the skills of those who had the passion to put their all into the project, rather than simply be paid hirelings. And the public too — the richest of them — to fund a large proportion of it. To share the blame, should it all come to nought.

Following through obsessions was second nature to him, but also was a dead end once fulfilled. Megan, his Welsh wife, was a perfect example. An exemplary singer, she had charmed her way into his heart first from the radio and then from his bedside. His pursuit of her mimicked the classic novels he had read as a child, and she, in turn, had hardly been an easy fish to catch. Yet, as soon as he possessed her, the obsession itself ran to ground. Now the most he saw of her was across the room at parties.

Wilhelm wasn't a religious man, and his lack of conviction to buy into any promise of afterlife drove him to make so much of the reality he lived and breathed. However, religious imagery had to come from somewhere, and the human mind was as good a source as any. So, when he had researched the legends of Hollow Earth, read the accounts of Olaf Jansen, and delved into the Tibetan legend of Agharta, it wasn't that difficult to become obsessed by the notion that a possible Garden of Earth set within

Earth actually existed. And whilst there was no promise of eternal life to be had from this utopia, the reports of inhabitants living to the age of *hundreds* was not to be sniffed at.

He wasn't vain, but he had lived a full and well-deserved life, and didn't consider that he wanted to give it up any time soon. His other research project, the charity *Immortality*, was also dedicated to finding answers for a subject which the general human race seemed happy to kick under the carpet. But nothing comes to those who do not seek, and he knew he *really* would be wasting his money if an answer was out there and he *didn't* search for it.

He glanced through the emails, deleting the obvious spam, and decided to read through the others properly when he had more time. Sitting back in his leather chair he buzzed for his secretary. Another obsession, a voyeuristic one, although she was strictly eye candy only. Wilhelm considered himself quite moral, but also knew Megan would rip the financial heart out of him if he played around. And for the moment, he didn't want to.

Candice came quickly after his call. Dressed in a two-piece black suit, the formal clothing complemented her curves, clung so tight that it almost undressed her as it dressed her. Her natural blonde hair was tightly tied back in a pony tail, while a black headband kept her fringe out of her eyes. Wilhelm found himself wondering whether her lingerie was also black.

"Candice, what appointments have I got today?"

Both of them knew that he already knew.

She flipped open her palm top and ran through his schedule. He was fascinated by new technology, yet simultaneously confounded by it. If mankind could produce such a thing, could send satellites into the farthest reaches of space, could replicate most of the devices from those old James Bond and SF movies, and — godamnit — find time to put impressions of bears onto toilet paper, then why hadn't it properly addressed the issue of mortality?

It was all surface, that was the problem. Papering over the cracks of age, rather than getting to the nub of it.

He watched as Candice closed the palm top.

"Will that be all?"

Was it his imagination, or was Candice lingering?

"Yes, that's all."

She turned on her heel like a pirouetting ballerina and left the room, her spike leaving an indentation in the carpet.

Wilhelm stared at that mark for a very long time.

TWO

The morning passed uneventfully, meetings came and went where his presence was required but not his personality. He idly considered whether a holographic image would have sufficed. Finally, after an extended luncheon, he found himself back in his office around four in the afternoon. He sent Candice home for the avoidance of even a modicum of temptation, and read through the emails he had received about Hollow Earth.

He started with those of his project organiser, Robbie McGuffin. They had managed to get another scientist on board, and his credentials appeared to check out even though Wilhelm was more than aware how such details could be faked. None of the government-employed scientists would have anything to do with him, and he wouldn't have been surprised if his contact with them had been passed onto various world security forces to monitor his activities. It wouldn't have been the first time he had been under *investigation*.

There were a few other emails and pieces of admin that he gave a cursory glance to and put aside for another day. Amongst those were two emails from a Richard Dean which didn't initially catch his eye, but then their duality concentrated his mind and he decided to read them.

The earlier email appeared to be a response to their automated 'welcome' information, being titled *Re: Thank you for your Hollow Earth interest*, but the second had been flagged urgent, subjected *Can you help us?*

Wilhelm opened the earlier email first. It was intriguing in itself. He hadn't heard the legend of the green children and would normally have dismissed it out of hand if Richard hadn't suggested that his wife, Julia, was a descendent. However, this on its own also wouldn't have held his interest for too long. The email was rather flippant, written in haste and without much thought. It smacked of insincerity, and Wilhelm was nothing if not sincere.

The second email, however, sent approximately a day after the first, was another matter. Unbelievably it suggested that Hollow Earth denizens had abducted Richard's daughter. Wilhelm would have laughed if the tone hadn't been so serious, if the email hadn't been ridden with panic that leapt from the screen. And as he read the account several times he gained less of an impression of a hoax, and more of a glimmer of opportunity. Something else also suggested the veracity of the comments, which was connected to Wilhelm's personal situation.

Apparently, according to Richard, he and his wife had been downstairs when they heard a noise from the child's bedroom. Having raced upstairs he'd seen an open window, with the missing child hauled across the fields at the rear of the property. It was dark, but the abductors were described as short and stumpy, travelling at a speed that belied their size.

Having immediately contacted the police no trace of the abductors could be found, however a full investigation was underway. Again, this didn't hold Wilhelm's attention and only seemed to add to a hoax, but further down a revelation appeared which rooted the happening in the every day.

"And at the bottom of all this," Richard wrote, "I now find that my wife has hidden something from me which might well prove relevant. She has an obsessive-compulsive disorder, but she doesn't believe it to be such. She actually considers that her *rituals* have been what have kept our family safe. Normally I'd be dismissive of this, apart from suggesting she seek treatment of course, but following Holly's disappearance she tells me that another relative of hers holds the same belief.

"I know how this sounds. I know how implausible this is. But with the green children reference I mentioned in my other email — which is copied in below should you have deleted it — and the compulsive behaviour which appears to be generational, I wondered whether you'd come across anything similar when researching your expedition. Not that I'm expecting anything to come of this, but my wife is hysterical and I'm clutching at straws. The police are doing what they can, but it isn't enough. I can't believe it myself, and no doubt this will be deleted unread, but if you have any information please pass it on."

Wilhelm left the email open, read and re-read it again. He had heard of rumours of the inhabitants of Hollow Earth who weren't always as benevolent as he had been led to believe. Yet this email had caused him to evaluate two things. Firstly, this jaunt of his had suddenly taken on a reality that he hadn't been sure of before. It was one thing to postulate and speculate, and quite another for the word to be made flesh. If he was to take Richard's account as fact, then maybe there was truth in the legends after all. Of course, there was still no proof in it, but there was one thing which pressed on him to believe. And that was the second point: Megan, his wife, also suffered from OCD.

THREE

He decided to respond to Richard's email. To obtain more information about the genetic line. In his first missive, Richard had been adamant there were no male heirs in his family, and that was certainly the case with Megan. But also Richard had mentioned he had traced several generations of the family, and if he was correct about his theory then several hundreds of people around the world might be affected. It wasn't implausible that Megan could also be descended from that green child.

He wasn't foolish, Richard might have been thorough with his research, but if a file was sent over containing a family tree and Megan's name was on it, then that would be something to conjure with. He could employ his own staff to work back from it, to unsettle any information which might be false, and to determine whether there was any truth in the matter.

Even as he clicked *send* he did so with a feeling of despondency, that either way the situation was turning bad. But it was too late to stop it, and deciding to assuage himself a moment he searched the BBC news websites for details of a missing girl, to see whether the official line might back up Richard's story.

And indeed, he found what he was looking for. Again, he was caught between the nature of truth and lies, of fiction and reality. He *knew* that the major governments believed in the existence of Hollow Earth, that their Illuminati were cognisant of it. Could it simply be that this story was sent to wrong foot him. Was it possible that all these links were just false?

To bolster his confidence he re-read reports he had been sent about the Earth being hollow, traced back his enthusiasm and wiped the disagreeable itch of hoax from his head. He wasn't getting any younger, that was the bottom line. He just wasn't getting any younger.

One question that had been raised by some of the scientists who had *declined* his invitations was how a Hollow Earth accounts for gravity. They claimed that the earth would not contain enough matter to produce the gravity we experience on its surface, and that if the earth were hollow then each inhabitant would be floating inside in zero gravity.

Yet *his* scientists' calculations concluded that Newtonian gravity could be consistent with a Hollow Earth. That a Hollow Earth could feasibly contain all of the estimated mass *and* be able to exert the surface accumulation of gravity seen on the outer surface.

Not only that, but there was plenty of evidence to suggest that all other planets, and even the sun, were hollow.

How was that so? Well, the sun has an electromagnetic field caused by the rotation of its crystal shell about its inner sun. But, if the sun were a gaseous planet it could not produce such a field. As astronomers believe stars are gaseous and planets have molten interiors they cannot explain the observed magnetic fields in suns or planets. Skylab photography revealed that the nuclear reactions on the sun emanate from permanent stationary *nuclear cells*. Such permanency strongly indicates that the surface of the sun is solid, not liquid nor gaseous. In fact, Skylab discovered that the sun has permanent coronal holes at its poles taken in X-ray, and ultra violet images could also indicate it has polar openings.

Taken as fact, this discovery that the Sun has a solid surface would have to be the greatest landmark in hollow planets' research in decades. Because if the Sun has a solid surface then this can only mean one thing - that the Sun is hollow, because the Sun does not have enough mass to be solid all the way through. If the Sun has a solid surface, the Sun would have to be hollow.

By recalculating the planets and sun's masses assuming that the greatest portion of their mass is in an inner shell, all would have solid surfaces - thus making it possible that these planets can generate the magnetic fields they have been observed to have. But also making it possible that they were hollow within the shell.

That was how it had been explained to Wilhelm, and it seemed just as plausible as the arguments against it. And if the inside of the earth was hollow, and purported to be akin to a Garden of Eden, then what of the inhabitants?

Here opinion was equally divided. In some instances they were a superior race, who regularly sent 'spaceships' into the outer world to monitor mankind. After all, the survival of the planet depended on what we were doing to it. Wilhelm considered himself forward-thinking in this regard, and had long ago implemented 'green' thinking within his businesses, albeit if he hadn't totally understood the meaning of the term and had been doing so to impress cultural partners. In this version of events, the world was like H.G.Wells' *Time Machine* in reverse. With the Eloi on the inside of the world and the destructive and backward Morlock on the outside. But of course, that was a fiction; yet also it seemed, was the alternative theory.

That had been propagated by Ray Palmer, editor of the *Amazing Stories* magazine back in the mid-1940s, having received a document from the writer Richard Sharpe Shaver titled *A Warning To Future Man*. Ostensibly fiction, Palmer expanded the original manuscript himself and presented it as faction. Shaver wrote of extremely advanced pre-historic races who had built cavern cities inside Earth before abandoning us for another planet due to damaging radiation from the Sun. Those ancients also abandoned some of their offspring here, a minority of whom remained noble and human 'Teros', while most degenerated over time into a population of mentally impaired sadists known as 'Deros' -short for 'detrimental robots.' Shaver's 'robots' were not mechanical constructs, but were robot-like due to their savage behaviour.

According to Shaver, these Deros still lived in the cave cities, kidnapping surface-dwelling people by the thousands for meat or torture. They were also known to use 'flying saucers' to make these sorties, and other parallels in other stories gave them equal status for Hollow Earth devotees. Until now, Wilhelm's hopes had been for the peaceable Eden-dwellers, but Richard's description of the kidnap of his daughter made him shudder. Could it be that all the stories were correct, that good and bad existed within Hollow Earth just as it existed here?

A vein pulsed at the side of Wilhelm's head, giving him a brief moment of excruciating pain. He had been experiencing similar symptoms of late and strove to disregard it, whilst at the same time he couldn't deny that he had fears about his health.

He sighed, loudly. Outside his plate glass window overlooking Oslo harbour the sun was already setting. He checked his watch.

It was almost nine o'clock. He couldn't believe he had sat there conjugating for such a length of time, yet the evening's work had proved much more useful than that accomplished during the day. He wondered whether he should sell all his businesses, create more time for himself and other issues. People knew of his obsession even if they didn't know the depth of it. Rivals were poised to use it at any time to unthrone him, and members of his own company were no doubt plotting behind his back. He just needed to focus, to take some time to consider the things that mattered, doing everything at once just led to overload.

He was about to close down his computer when another email arrived from Richard in response to the one he had sent earlier. As requested, a PDF file was attached containing the family tree so far. Wilhelm opened it, and whilst Megan wasn't mentioned he decided to print it and take it home. Maybe this would lead nowhere after all, but a sensation at the back of his mind suggested otherwise.

FOUR

He tended to drive nowadays, instead of employing a chauffeur. Pleasures were rare and being behind a wheel was one of them. As he headed along Frognerstranda he contemplated the remainder of Richard's email. The plea for assistance, the confirmation that the police still had no further clues as to the missing child. Holly had been Richard's first born, Wilhelm and Megan had no children — he had others from a previous marriage, but that was incidental. He began to consider the disappearance around the world of other first born children, the case of Madeleine McCann being a high profile example. Conjecture was anything. However many dots you made on a piece of paper, without fail you would be able to join them up.

Richard had also mentioned that subject to the kidnap he had been able to contact other members of Julia's family, whether by tenacity on his part or the fact that they had come to him. All of them apparently had some form of OCD. All of them had it passed down to them by their mother's. And all of their mother's were now dead. Needless to say, all of those affected had been the first born child.

His fingers drummed the steering wheel as he turned onto Nylandsveien. As he thought before, joining dots was easy. What wasn't always easy was knowing the shape they would make.

Megan was home when he arrived. An uncorked bottle of wine, half-empty, was in the kitchen and she was slumped on the sofa in front of the plasma screen in the living area. The screen was the focal point even when it was off, although neither of them really watched it. He glanced over towards her, noticed that her glass had slipped from her hand and there was another stain on the carpet which would need cleaning. He sighed. It wasn't an uncommon occurrence.

As she was sleeping he decided to check in her bathroom. Normally she refused him entry, they each had individual bathrooms and it had been a long time since he had soaped her back — or her front. This was her den, the place where she shut herself away when her OCD behaviour was at its worst. He expected that was more frequently than she let on, considering the extent of her condition as it was known to him.

Without fail the bathroom was spotless, and this evening was no exception. The white surfaces gleamed, the taps shone, and there wasn't a hair to be seen trapped in the plughole. Naturally they had a cleaning lady for the rest of the house, but this room was out of bounds to her. It was a sizeable room, with three separate cabinets. In one of them, Megan kept all her cleaning products, specifically used by her in this room only. The other two cabinets contained the familiar items you would find in any bathroom — toothpaste, cotton buds, tampons, shampoo, tweezers, and an assortment of medicines. The quirk being that both cabinets contained exactly the same items in exactly the same positions. Even the squeeze on the toothpaste was measured out as identically as possible each time she cleaned her teeth. He had once asked her how she had coped when she was a singer, travelling the road, but she said she had only begun this behaviour since her mother's death.

What had pleased him was that she had been open about it right from the start, although considering the set-up he supposed that she had to be. Naturally his assumption was that it was the death which had kicked off the obsession, and whilst she didn't resist his intervention and appointments with their GP, he also felt that she didn't want to be treated either. So, he let it be. If it comforted her, then who was he to stop that? And on the one occasion where he had become infuriated, and invaded her space and started throwing things around, she had become so desolate and hysterical that he knew tampering wasn't the answer.

So, like the general deterioration of the marriage, he let it slide.

With an ear to the living room he checked out the bathroom cabinets. He didn't have to examine them too carefully to know they were pristine. Everything lined up soldier fashion, twinned and perfect. He slid them closed, careful not to leave any fingerprints on the glass, and shut the door carefully behind him.

Returning to where Megan slouched on the sofa he crouched

down beside her and held her hand. It was warm, and her cheeks were flushed red from the wine. Guilt stirred within him. It shouldn't be like this, yet he was so busy. There wasn't always time...

She opened her eyes and spread a smile.

"I feel sick."

"Sit up, you'll feel better."

"I'll be ok."

He eased her into a sitting position, then sat on the sofa beside her.

"I didn't have much wine you know, just half a bottle."

"And half of *that* seems to be on the carpet."

She looked sheepish. Mumbled a *sorry*.

"It's fine. We need new carpet in here anyway."

He sat back and cradled her head in his hands. It felt good. Although just for a moment a despairing sadness swept through him, as though he were on the brink of losing her, and until then hadn't appreciated what she meant to him.

If only he could be sure that she felt the same way.

"Is everything ok?"

She nodded. "Yes, why?"

"The glass, the bottle."

"The difference?"

He shrugged. "My concern?"

She laughed. "Yes, everything is ok. Just fancied a night in, you know. Thinking about the past."

"Any regrets?"

"Not really, no. Why do you ask?"

"Because you're my wife."

She smiled again; appeared about to say something, then thought better of it and closed her eyes.

"I'm tired."

"Can I show you something?"

"Bit late for that, isn't it?"

"Pardon?"

"Nothing." She sat up a little straighter. "What is it?"

Wilhelm reached into his pocket and pulled out the family tree he had printed from the computer. "This has been presented to me and I was curious. I haven't done any of this research myself, but I'd like your opinion. See if anything is familiar to you."

She took the paper from him, unfolded it. Then leant over to the side table and turned on the light.

"Is this my family tree?"

"I don't know. You're not on it."

She traced her manicured finger along several of the lines. "I don't know any of these names."

"They go back a long way, several hundred years, I'm not expecting you to."

"Why do you think this has anything to do with me?"

"Just a hunch. Keep looking."

"There is a group here that came out of Wales. The writing is so small though, I can hardly read it."

"I had to reduce it in order to print it."

She held it closer to the light. "Well, the line ends here, with a family holding the surname of Jones. Their first names match those of my grandparents, but my mother wasn't a Jones as you know. It could be anyone, really."

Wilhelm held his breath for a moment. "What if I were to tell you that several of those on that list suffer from OCD?"

"Really?"

"Really."

"Then I wouldn't know what to say."

He took the paper from her and kissed her fingers. "Who are you protecting?"

"Why, I'm protecting you Wilhelm. You know that, we've been through this before."

"Even though we've been distant?"

"Even though we've been distant."

He kissed her lips this time. "Let me take you to bed."

She did, willingly.

Come morning, they were on a plane.

JULIA

ONE

Julia fidgeted nervously. She hated big occasions, and was on edge, at breaking point. Five days had passed since Holly's disappearance, without any inroads having been made by the police. Richard had been adamant to the point of obsession that this was linked to his *Green* discovery, and fear told her that he was probably right.

That evening itself was a blur. She remembered waking and finding it unusual that Richard wasn't in bed; then coming downstairs to watch over his shoulder as her Lalique cabinet flew open. It was at that moment, she knew, they were most vulnerable, and an ominous presence of dread had filled her completely. When Richard told her Holly had gone she could do little but nod in acknowledgement. The hysteria, rage, and frustration all came several hours later, as, with Poppy hugged to her breast, she sobbed violently, feeling that her life had been torn away from her.

Naturally that feeling remained. But what felt equally horrific was the amount of media attention poured on them as a couple. Only now did that seem to abate, although her emotions were so mixed she wasn't sure if it was a blessing or a curse. Certainly it increased the possible success of finding Holly, but equally she needed space to breathe again.

Richard had advised her to contact Ann the day after the kidnap. She knew better than to argue, and anyway the thought had been hovering in her own mind. Now that familial connection had escalated: within a few minutes she would be addressing fifteen strangers, all linked by blood, on the subject of her rituals that she had held so dear. She felt raw, exposed, but in a sense comforted. Within the group were two other women who had also experienced losses. Two other children who had disappeared out of sight.

They were in the back garden and the morning was bright, sunny. It was the only place where all the guests could be accommodated. They wanted to keep it as low key as possible. A few chairs were dotted about, but most would have to stand. Richard was inside with some of the men who had accompanied their partners. Wilhelm, the Norwegian businessman was also there, who Richard had communicated with over the Internet. Julia wasn't convinced that he could help them, but she couldn't deny his presence. In any event, his wife might be family too, although it had yet to be confirmed.

Whether Megan was or was not related, however, seemed immaterial since she also suffered from OCD. It was a fact that Julia was in two minds about understanding. All female members of the same family having the same condition could only point to the veracity of her rituals. She felt validated, yet at the same time afraid. Because they weren't working, were they? The rituals. If they had been then Holly would be here.

She had met Megan the previous day. They had sat alone in her living room and talked quietly about their rituals, about how their mothers had insisted on their importance, and how they both shared the ritual counting even though their specific rituals were different. Each were concerned with the same thing, however: items had to be kept in place. Megan was obviously finding it hard being away from her bathroom, and only the knowledge that the door had been locked and nothing could be disturbed had enabled her to make the journey. Yet when Julia had mentioned how her figurines had moved of their own account Megan needed calming. The knowledge that she was childless only vaguely tempering her fears.

From the emails sent by those who were now congregating in her garden, Julia knew that they were also first born children. And the two children that had gone missing — both daughters — were first born too. Julia hadn't found this surprising in itself. Her mother had instilled her in the importance of the first born carrying on the ritual. But then, it hadn't quite been like that either. Her rituals had come from within her, hadn't they; they had developed as she had developed. Not simply out of mimicry but something more innate. It had only been her mother who then nurtured and supported them, just as she had been planning to do with Holly.

At the thought of her daughter tears pricked the corners of her eyes. It was all so desperate, she wasn't sure how she was holding it together. It was only the tenacity of needing to keep to those rituals which had focussed her over the past few days. Now Richard knew, she could rely on him to support her, to give her the space for what needed to happen.

Megan smiled from across the garden, she was chatting to an elderly relative — Julia found it natural to call them relatives, even though she had none before. She found her presence reassuring. As she did of Ann, who was with the two women whose daughters had gone missing. Everyone else seemed distant, unsure, certainly out of their comfort zones. She felt her recent loss somehow marked her as an outsider, so that she was still looking in rather than participating. When it came to the other women with lost children, a couple of months separated them from their disappearances. She recalled hearing about one of them on the news.

If there were any assurances to be had it was that those children hadn't been found. She hung onto the hope that Holly was alive. At an atomic level she was sure she would know if she was dead.

Birds flitted about the garden, sparrows and blue tits. A light breeze carried motion into Holly's swing at the far end. The grass needed cutting, Richard had originally promised to do this at the weekend. There was a semblance of normality which frightened her, which was suggestive of a world below that in which they were living. It was all surface, no shine. Strip away the routines, the rituals, the things you take for granted, and there were hard certainties which she didn't want to view.

Richard left the confines of the house and approached her over the grass.

"Everyone's here who said they'd be here. Are you ok?"

She slipped her arm around his. "I think so. I still can't understand any of this."

"None of us can. But we can only deal with what we know. However improbable it all sounds. We have to pool our resources."

She allowed herself a smile. "You sound so bureaucratic, Richard, as though you're back in the business world again."

He shrugged. "Is that a good thing?"

"I need an anchor right now. And yes, it is."

She turned to address the crowd. From the terrace Wilhelm clapped his hands quickly, and silence fell across the garden. As people turned towards him he nodded his head over at Julia. Taking a deep breath, she began to talk.

"I know this is as hard for you to understand as it is for me, but you're all aware of the situation with my daughter Holly and some of you have also been plunged to the same depths as us. Regardless of what we know, we have to accept that we're all related, all first born daughters with rituals, just fifteen of us here but more than a hundred across the world. And, if my husband is correct, all descended from a little girl who was discovered not more than fifty miles from here. A girl who proclaimed that she had come from under the earth.

"I know this sounds nonsensical, but if you're like me then you'll need to believe some truth in it. How do I know? Well, the discovery of *you*, of a whole hidden community of one family with similar rituals must give validity to what has been happening. I know from some of you that your rituals have been disrupted of late. Those of you with children will also be sharing my concern. I'm not entirely sure what we *can* do, but what we *can't* do is sit by and just let these things happen. We perform our rituals for a reason, and if they're not working we must pool together to change that. I need something to keep Holly safe. I need you."

Her voice broke on the last three words, and she turned towards Richard to hide her tears. Nevertheless, she also felt proud. She had set out her stall as forcibly as she could, and until doing so hadn't had the belief she was capable of it.

Richard carried on her message beside her.

"What we're saying is that we're facing the unknown. We're not suggesting some kind of vigilante force separate from that of the police. They have their methods but we'll have ours. If we're wrong, if we've overblown the situation into something that it isn't, then we're not going to do any harm by the methods we're proposing. But if we're right, then maybe we *can* make a difference. Maybe all of you have a purpose and the time has come to do something."

As Julia listened she knew he sounded overdramatic. What did they know after all? But still, there was a tug inside her similar to a compass, pointing her in the right direction. She *knew* that they were part of something else, and despite all the fibres in her body wishing to believe otherwise, she knew they had to go with this. Holly's life could be at stake, after all.

Someone spoke up from the crowd. "But what is it that you want us to do."

Wilhelm's booming voice overtook Richard's answer. "Your rituals aren't working as individuals. You need to pool them to make them stronger. We're proposing that those who wish to, should remain in the local area. Select a new ritual, a new focus which all of you can participate as a group. That should strengthen the defences. My wife, Megan, will be part of that. And whilst you're doing that, we're going in."

"Going in? Going in where?"

Julia couldn't place the speaker, but the anxiety in her voice was shared by all of them.

"Into the earth. Our Hollow Earth. We're going in to get your children back."

TWO

Julia had mixed feelings about Wilhelm. He had quickly taken charge, although she couldn't help but feel he had his own agenda. Still, he was not only a force to be reckoned with, but a voice to be listened to. As he had detailed his plan, backed up with all the knowledge of the supposed Hollow Earth that he had accumulated over several years, his beliefs had washed over them. Like a navy shirt placed in a tub of white clothes, they came out of it coloured, his message getting to the heart of them, and within each of them — she knew — they believed it.

Perhaps she would have believed less if it wasn't for Megan. As they chatted after the meeting, eating sausage rolls and sandwiches as if they were at a garden party or wake, she felt a kinship towards her that she hadn't known before. Megan put her at ease, without her really knowing why.

"Wilhelm is a great man," Megan was saying. "Admittedly we were drifting apart, but the qualities which drew me to him are still there. He has a magnetic personality, confirmed beliefs, and a passion which I find particularly alluring. Of course," she winked, "he's ridiculously rich as well, but I find that to be a bonus rather than an incentive."

"And these Hollow Earth stories?"

She paused, choosing her words. "It's long been an obsession, but I can't argue against that, can I? Wilhelm keeps his cards close to his chest sometimes. I haven't been privy to everything. But I will say this, if he wants to do something then he'll do it, and if there is any truth in those stories he'll be the one to find out."

"Richard wants to go with him."

"Richard wants to *do something*. I find that admirable in a man." Julia nodded. "So do I."

"Listen," Megan said, "until Holly is found we just have to run with this. You and I — and those women out there who are staying with us — know that we're doing these rituals for a purpose. Wilhelm paid for all sorts of therapy for me believing I had some kind of psychological disorder, but one email from your Richard and he's changed his mind. We know we do this for a reason, but previously we might not have been sure what that was.

Just imagine, if all the descendants from that green child have OCD and are protecting their families then what are they protecting them from? I shudder to think, but I want to be involved when it happens."

"Some of those other women are going back home."

"And they have a right to. They're scared. They have their own families and their familiar rituals and they feel they can do more good at home rather than here. But more will join us — don't you feel it? Once word gets around. There's safety in numbers, after all."

Julia sighed. "All I want is my daughter back. This is a nightmare, everything's running out of control."

"And control is what we're about. Control is what we're good at. We've got to keep focussed, Julia, for our sakes if not for anything else."

"You seem so calm."

"I'm a swan. Underneath the surface, my legs are going crazy."

Julia nodded. If there was an analogy for her then it would be jelly. She felt sick. If any swimming was to be done then it was in her head. For a moment she reached out, steadied herself on Megan's arm. *Sorry*, she breathed. Then feeling embarrassed, she saw Richard enter the house and decided to follow. She made her excuses from Megan, but halfway across the garden, Ann intercepted her. Concern written all over her face.

"I'm worried, Julia, I'm worried we're focussing everything on ourselves."

"Have you heard from Susan, in America?"

"Yes, she's fine. At the moment. But she's my first born, as you know. If there *is* something in this then it will be her, won't it, rather than me who they'll go for. They're stopping the evolutionary line."

"We don't know that."

"Can't you feel it? I could tell that you knew there was something wrong when you were at my house the other day. The fact that we both had our rituals. The fact that we're in touch right now. It's all building to a crescendo, isn't it?"

"We've got to remain calm, Ann. I thought you were holding it together."

"It's all a façade. I've been like the Dutch boy with his finger in the dam for over twenty years, all that pressure, all the belief that I was in this alone. Now suddenly everything's come to a head and I just want to let go, to release it all, to have nothing more to do with it."

Julia looked at her, shocked. Ann had seemed such a calming influence a few days ago, but she understood. If they weren't careful, a feeling of hopelessness — not just of the future, but of all the rituals undertaken in the past — could pervade them. Without needing the strength to fight for her daughter, Julia might well start to crumble the same way.

"I mean," Ann continued, "all of you are here now. Is there any need for me?"

"You know there is. Well, to the extent that we know anything at all, which we don't."

She gave Ann a hug, and had the feeling it would be the first of many. Everything was so tenuous wasn't it? This grip on the boundary between reality and fantasy. Even what we considered was 'real' sounded fantastic when you realised we were all on a ball spinning through limitless space.

"There's something else," Ann said, "several of my clocks were wrong this morning. Not just the wrong times, but the hands were bent. I don't know if I'm gonna be able to set them again."

"Stay here," Julia said, "you know we're going to pool our resources. You don't have to go back there. We can create new rituals, new ways to keep everything at bay. Until, at least, we're clear what's going on."

Ann nodded. Some of her resolve seemed to have returned. "Sorry," she said, "I feel a little silly now."

"Don't be. These are hard times for all of us, believe me."

"Yes, of course. I just feel so helpless. I've never had that feeling before, I've always been in control."

Julia forced a smile. "I know. It's ok. Listen, I have to go and talk to Richard. I'll be back in a moment."

Ann nodded again, and impulsively gave Julia another hug. However as Julia walked away she knew that they were only touching the surface. Things were going to get a lot more frantic before they got better, if they ever did. Would they actually be able to hold all this together?

The events of the previous few days had passed like a dream. She was sleepwalking through this, her only defence mechanism. And she knew what the others were thinking. What about their children? What about the safety of their rituals? Nobody held certainties any more.

Richard was talking animatedly amongst a group of men, the partners of those in the garden. They looked like a mob. She imagined them picking up pitchforks and burning torches, storming wherever they felt needed to be stormed. Perhaps they were right, perhaps the time for rituals had passed and action now needed to be taken.

But, she also wondered, was it just their imaginations which were getting out of hand. Could Holly's disappearance be linked to something much more usual, although just as frightening? Richard and Wilhelm seemed hell bent on pursuing the Hollow Earth theory, but it just couldn't be correct, could it? All the same, she wished that was the truth.

Holly disappearing into a fantasyworld was much more palatable than the real world. She had been shielding her from the real world for much of her life, hadn't she?

Richard caught her eye. He made his excuses with the group and came over, adding another hug to her day.

"How's it going?"

She shrugged. "It's just *going*. Isn't it? Nowhere fast."

"Come on, chin up. We're going to beat this."

"Do you really think so."

"I have to."

She smiled. "Are you turning out to be the man I've always wanted you to be?"

He frowned. "What does that mean?"

"Nothing. Sorry. So, what's the plan?"

"Wilhelm is making enquiries about getting us over to the Arctic Circle. A couple of the men want to come, those who have also lost children, although the others prefer to stay with their wives. Apparently he has a Russian icebreaker at his disposal; we might have to cut through the ice."

"Holly didn't disappear in the Arctic, did she?"

"Well, no. That has to be somewhere local. But as Wilhelm says, it could be anywhere. At least there's existing information about an entrance in the Arctic."

"Richard, just listen to yourself. Even if there is an entrance

Holly would be several thousand miles from it. We've got to look locally."

"I don't know. Wilhelm seems convinced..."

"Look. Wilhelm has his own interests at heart. Don't get me wrong, Megan is a lovely woman, but this has been his bugbear for a few years. He's got motivation to get going because of us, but it means nothing. He has the money, but he really knows no more than any of us. Holly is our priority, nothing else. I'm all for staying here as a group of women with our rituals, trying to prevent further kidnappings, but for you to go to the Arctic seems nonsensical. I thought you were going to look in Woolpit."

She felt a hand on her shoulder, and turned to find Wilhelm standing behind her.

"Julia, we can either go looking where we know there is an entrance, or go looking where we don't know there is an entrance. We can get to the Arctic in two days. The ship is ready. It's always been ready. I've just been waiting for the opportunity — some would say excuse — to make that journey. Now I have the courage of my convictions."

"It just seems so far-fetched."

"And maybe it is. Maybe it's a spiral. But you have the police for the regular investigation. And I know Richard can't sit still whilst they go about *their* business."

A pocket of rage formed inside her. She counted under her breath to control it, even as she pondered its effectiveness.

"And what about Poppy?" Through gritted teeth.

"Poppy will be safe. She isn't the first born."

It was too much. Julia felt her legs give way and she slipped in slow motion to the floor.

THREE

The following day plans had been finalised and put into action. Richard gave her a long, lingering kiss as he left for the airport with Wilhelm and two other men. There was an aura of unreality, and Julia had to remind herself that this was actually happening. Whilst Richard hadn't convinced her the Arctic was necessary, she had conceded that he was determined to go. Just like her, he believed he was protecting his family.

After feeding Poppy and placing her carrycot beside the sofa, she opened the door to Megan, Ann, and a few of the other women who had decided to stay locally. Within thirty minutes the ritual they had decided on had begun.

It was quite simple, like a round of perpetual prayer but lacking religious overtones. The one commonality between them was the counting regime. The *calming* ritual rather than the *order* ritual. There were those like Julia who maintained a precision with regards to ornaments, those who obsessively cleaned, those who kept clocks, those who had to touch door handles in a certain order, those who continuously kept lists. Yet all of those rituals took place within a home, which precluded them from working as a group. And with the disruption of some of their individual rituals, a group ritual, a common ritual, seemed the way forwards.

They sat in a circle for convenience. They had agreed to perform for two hours a day — one hour in the morning and the other late afternoon. Success could only be judged by the absence of failure, but they knew this. They had known it all their adult lives.

Julia began.

One. One two three. Two. One two three. Three. One two three.

One. One two three. Two. One two three. Three. One two three.
One. One two three. Two. One two three. Three. One two three.
Megan took over.
One. One two three. Two. One two three. Three. One two three.
One. One two three. Two. One two three. Three. One two three.
One. One two three. Two. One two three. Three. One two three.
Then Ann. Then Judy, who had lost her eldest daughter, Claire, two months ago. The family hadn't seen the abductor. It had happened during the early hours of the morning. Again, an open window and no trace, save for their youngest daughter waking to see a shadow disappear. Then Mary, whose only daughter had been taken seven weeks ago. Once more, similar circumstances, but on this occasion as she returned home from school.

One. One two three. Two. One two three. Three. One two three.
One. One two three. Two. One two three. Three. One two three.
One. One two three. Two. One two three. Three. One two three.

Like a chant, like a mantra. Between them they could feel the room filling with power. Slowly at first, then more palpable until the curtains seemed to wave with static electricity, and goosebumps rose on each and every arm. And as these outward manifestations increased, so did the belief and commitment within the group.

A surge of purpose ran through Julia. She knew, without a shadow of a doubt, that what they were doing was correct. That it would bring results. If the faith in her rituals had taken a knock following Holly's disappearance then it was back again now. Holly going was *not* her fault. She had kept a tangle of guilt inside her since she disappeared, but she knew now that she couldn't have avoided it. What had happened was that those who threatened the safety of her family had become stronger, rather than her becoming weaker. But now the power was back in their hands again, working together might really make a difference.

Of course, the 'who' and the 'why' of it was a mystery, but she was now convinced it was linked to the green heritage. More emails and telephone calls had come through overnight. Each of her ancestors practised rituals, and more of them were coming to assist. Some of those had also experienced disruptions. Presumably their secrets, their daughters, were hidden inside the earth; and however fantastical that sounded, Julia knew it was the truth.

What was it Sherlock Holmes had said, through Conan Doyle? That once you eliminate the impossible, whatever remains, no matter how improbable, must be the truth. She felt that was as sure as anything right now.

The round came back to her. She slipped into it easily, found that she didn't have to concentrate. It was second-nature, but not simply because she had practised it before, it had become natural within the current situation. As she finished, she suddenly became aware of a memory that couldn't be hers. She was sitting on a dirt floor, within a circular building, the chanting of others resonated the walls. Looking up, she saw a conical roof with an opening towards the sky. It reminded her of a church, but it wasn't like any church she had previously known. Suddenly, without a doubt, she knew this was St Martin's Land; but instead of faltering as she had when Richard had first mentioned it, she found strength. Looking around at the group, she could see they knew it too.

As the shared memory dissipated, the voices within the group rose. As one now, they performed the ritual simultaneously, as was needed to be done. Protection enfolded them, nurtured and revealed them. Just for a moment Julia looked from one face to another and was sure she could see a tint of green.

RICHARD

ONE

Richard hunched his shoulders, trying to keep warm as he stood on the deck of the icebreaker. His gloved hands were stuffed deep in his pockets, but his fingers felt like icicles. He knew it was a cliché, but clichés were often the most apt method of description. That was why they were clichés in the first place.

However it was no clichéd sight which greeted his vision from the ship. White and blue extended to the horizon. The sun's glare was so brilliant that he wore sunglasses. He normally hated them. He wanted to see the world as it was, not shrouded in grey; but here there was no option. It was quite possible to be blinded by the sun.

They had been travelling for two days. Having departed Murmansk, they travelled north through open ocean for about a thousand miles. Ice first started to appear in large quantities near the Russian-owned Franz Josef Land islands. Wilhelm had proclaimed that it was from these islands that the Norwegian fishermen, Olaf and Jens Jansen, sailed northeast in 1829 and accidentally discovered the north polar opening, apparently described in a book titled *The Smokey God*. Richard wouldn't have been surprised if Wilhelm didn't have a copy on board, he seemed able to quote from it verbatim.

Cutting through the arctic ice the journey became much slower. Their ship was large enough to carry a helicopter, which was used at times to scout over the ice to find trails of open water which might make their journey easier and faster. Wilhelm had offered to take them up in it, however Richard had yet to acquiesce. For the moment the sturdiness of the ship was preferable to the bug in the air.

Apparently the geographic North Pole was only two days away. The further they journeyed through the ice, the further Richard felt divorced from reality. The two men who had come with them, Henry and John, aside from the crew and scientists of course, were personable companions, but the stress of being away from home on what seemed increasingly like a fool's mission was taking its toll.

Back in England, embedded within the very real circumstances of Holly's disappearance, this journey's goal had seemed *more* than plausible, it was necessary. However actually being here was different. Devoid of an anchor to reality, surrounded by blue and white, he was drifting. Wilhelm was another matter.

What had seemed passionate when he first met him, what had seemed inspirational and positive, now seemed maniacal beyond reason. Wilhelm didn't need an excuse to be here — he could have come at any time. The fact that Holly had given him a reason had seemed admirable, now Richard felt it was a crusade. That his daughter was a pawn and no more. Increasingly, frustration began to build that he was wasting his time.

Using the ship's radio to contact Julia, however, he found that she was upbeat. Their rituals had power, she said, but her words only served to emphasise how far from reality they had travelled in the space of a week. He began to long, to dream, for the sanctity of his antique shop.

Wilhelm had addressed them the previous evening, resplendent in a dinner suit whilst they had huddled over their food. It wasn't that the ship was cold as such, but the omnipresent outside atmosphere had an *effect*. His voice had boomed along the dining room, touching both scientist and guest alike.

"Gentlemen, now we have reached the ice we are really on our way. My estimate is that we will enter the north polar opening going south on the 141st meridian from the geographic North Pole. Half the journey will be through ice before we reach the open ocean, then after the second half of the journey — almost 600 miles — we will reach the inner continent and our destination.

"Mirages of this continent have been sighted all around the arctic for centuries. Admiral Peary sighted it northwest of Ellesmere Island on the northern shores of Canada in 1909 on his way to the pole. He named it Crockerland, believing it to be real. Dr Cook in 1906 saw it also northwest of his trek to the pole from Ellesmere Island and even took a picture of it as a background to his dogs and sledges. He named it Bradleyland. Captain Keenan sighted this land northwest of Harrison Bay, Alaska. The Russians have seen it north of the New Siberian Islands and named it Sannikov land. All these sightings of land in the arctic sea all point in one direction - to 141 E Longitude and 84.4 N Latitude, the coordinates where my scientists have triangulated the location of the north polar opening based on the direction that sightings of land mirages have been seen from all around the Arctic Ocean."

Richard cut into some pork, his knife cleanly separating it into two halves. When he put it into his mouth it was already cooling, almost cold.

Wilhelm continued: "It must be realised that in the arctic a mirage is the exact opposite of one in the desert. There, a hot layer of air rising from the surface looks like water, because it is reflecting the sky. In the arctic, warm air rising out of the polar opening heads high into the sky, and looking above you believe you see land. But of course, you *will* be seeing land, because the warm air will be reflecting the ground below. These phenomenon, as described by Peary, Cook, et al, are all proof that there is something out there; something just waiting to be discovered!"

Technical phrases ensued which Richard ducked out of, concentrating instead on his meal. Once he had finished, he looked around at the faces of the scientists. None of them inspired enthusiasm. Drop-outs one and all. He hadn't entered into conversation with anyone other than Henry and John, and even then it was strained. Just as he had looked up to Wilhelm as Holly's saviour, so similarly they had regarded him due to championing Wilhelm. Come the revolution, Richard might be strung up first.

TWO

On the fourth night his dreams were filled with stars. He was lying on his back, eyes open, looking upwards through a conical opening within a building of wattle and daub. Murmuring could be heard around him, but he wasn't inclined to turn his head. Instead he looked upwards, through the cone, and as he did so the night sky's expanse widened like an eye adjusting to the dark. Stars freckled the firmament, and he sought out the regular patterns: Orion's belt, the Great Bear, the Plough. Yet, try as he might they didn't reveal themselves, and as he regarded them more closely he realised that they were moving.

But of course, they weren't stars at all. He was within Hollow Earth and they couldn't exist there. What he saw were spaceships, tiny pinpricks of manufactured light ascending and descending.

As though he was being fed knowledge intravenously he

became aware their technology was far in advance of outer earth — several thousand years in fact. This explained the spaceships that ducked and dived like kites, performing manoeuvres that couldn't be replicated above ground. He was aware of other advances too, but the nature of these was beyond his understanding. Yet, if this was the case, then how did it explain the building he was within now?

He turned his head to the right. People arced around him, and when he looked left he saw the pattern was replicated. He was, in fact, within a semi-circle, and as he realised this the murmurings became more distinct. They were counting, in uniform, methodically and melodically. And with this realisation he knew the importance of the building. It was ancient, a focal point, a church for want of a better word. An oasis in a sea of technology.

The faces of those in the circle grew familiar. He recognised Ann, Megan, some of the other women who had answered his call. He scanned for Julia but couldn't find her, hoped that she was immediately behind him and tried to discern the timbre of her voice. Then the walls of the building dissolved and he found himself back on board the ship. He rubbed his eyes. Was he still asleep? He pinched himself and felt nothing, decided to force himself awake.

But he couldn't. Panicked seeped into him as he struggled to regain consciousness. He was aware, wasn't he, of his surroundings, down to the last nut and bolt in his room? So was he dreaming or not. Again, he struggled to push against an invisible barrier and finally broke through, wide-awake and gasping for air, as if surfacing from under water. He was freezing, his limbs were aching and his teeth were chattering. Yet the room was warm. It had been but a dream, nothing more, nothing less.

But the reality facing him was just as severe as the dream. He lay back and pulled the covers over his head, felt childish in doing so yet was comforted regardless. He had slept clothed and glanced at his watch. It was approaching five am. He wondered what Julia was doing now, if Poppy was sleeping ok. Perhaps they were in bed together, Poppy protectively held. He wondered if Julia's figurines had moved again.

The pressure in his head to achieve something was intense. This was why he was on the ship, and he *had* to trust in Wilhelm and his beliefs. Without that, he was nothing, had been sidetracked from the real issues, and he couldn't allow that belief. In some ways, his dream validated his role, whether imaginary or not. If there was something here, something close, then might it not be able to reach into his consciousness and let him know they were near? Hollow Earth didn't have to be the pull of demons, did it? There was good and bad on the surface, and no doubt that extended below. He *had* to believe in it, he would cry if he couldn't.

Wilhelm had intimated the previous evening that they might be close to the opening. Concern had been raised by Henry that if there was a hole in the Earth's surface then surely it would act as a plughole, spiralling the sea and the ship down into the earth. Wilhelm had responded with facts about the nature of gravity. That rather than gravity exerting its influence from the centre of the earth, science could prove that force comes from the surface not the core.

Richard wasn't convinced. How would they enter the hole? Wilhelm had suggested they would be welcomed, that ways would be made available to them. As far as Richard was concerned this meant Wilhelm didn't actually know. It wasn't as if he had been corresponding with any beings below the surface — if, indeed, they existed. All his evening speeches had been full of conjecture, relating on past accounts — some from centuries ago. For the first time when taking stock of his situation, enhanced with a frisson of fear which might have been a residue of the dream, Richard wondered whether his life could possibly be at stake. Whether he would drown in an ice-filled sea as the ship went down. Was his freezing waking state prescient?

Such conflicting thoughts entered his head as he settled back to sleep. Perhaps, just perhaps, it might be resolved in the morning.

THREE

When he awoke it was after nine and he'd missed breakfast. No doubt a sandwich could be rustled up for him, and he dressed quickly, wanting to see whether the landscape had changed.

Opening his cabin door he saw John and Henry in the hallway. Neither were clean-shaven, and neither looked like they had slept. He knew both of them had been drinking heavily the night before, presumably to chase out those demons threatening their lost children.

They regarded him nervously, and he realised they had been waiting for him. After what seemed an age, John spoke:

"Look, Richard, I don't know quite how to say this mate, but we've kind of trusted you on this and we're just wondering if... well, you know...just exactly what we might be getting into."

Richard was about to answer, realised he couldn't.

"We know you don't know all the answers," broke in Henry, "but after spending time with Wilhelm, we're just not sure of... how can I put this? His intentions."

"You see," said John, "what seemed like a good idea at the time, doesn't quite seem like it now, does it mate? Here we are, miles from our families, miles from anything. If it had just been him, like, then we wouldn't be here. Well, I know *I* wouldn't be here. But with you, with you it all made sense didn't it?"

Again, Richard found himself lost for words. How could he reassure them when he had been thinking the same thing? They had placed their trust in someone who was influential and had the resources to make promises he could keep — at least, as far as it came to finances. But if this was a misplaced mission, what of their children?

Flaps of reality peeled away from him as though he were being stripped bare. He was aware of Henry and John looking at him, curious as to what they really thought. He had to say *something*, didn't he? But before he could, there came a shout from the bridge.

"Land ahoy!"

Briefly Richard wondered whether that would be the correct terminology on a *proper* voyage, but the call galvanised them and they headed along the walkway to where Wilhelm was standing.

"Here," he said, breathless, "Here it is! We've arrived!"

Richard looked out over the expanse of ice and sea. Sunlight glinted off the landscape, as though a magnesium burn. He realised he had left his sunglasses down in his cabin, so squinted against the light. In the distance — exactly how far away was hard to judge — hovering over the sea was the semblance of a mirage. Greens and browns populated the sky, shapes which could have been buildings completed it. Was he looking at a shadow, or were his eyes playing tricks on him, making shapes out of nothing, drawing connections where nothing actually existed?

Wilhelm pounded him on the back. "It's it!" he kept repeating. "It's it."

Richard glanced across to John and Henry, who seemed transfixed by the scene, their concerns forgotten. Then he became aware that nearly everyone in the expedition was on deck, and almost simultaneously, as though it had emerged collectively rather than individually, a cheer rose up from the group, followed by applause. Everyone was beaming, from both excitement and relief; and Richard found that he was smiling too, pumping Wilhelm's hand as though Holly had already been found.

"We need to check this out," Wilhelm said. "Come with me to the helicopter Richard, we need an aerial view of this."

Richard nodded. His heart was pounding, empty stomach forgotten. He raced to his cabin and collected his sunglasses before heading up to the pad. Wilhelm was already on board, sitting next to the pilot. Two of the scientists were in the back, and Richard joined them. He'd not really exchanged words with them on the voyage, and they were talking animatedly to themselves, hardly acknowledging his presence. Again, he felt that his being there was almost incidental to the trip, that Holly's disappearance was simply the catalyst providing the impetus Wilhelm had been looking for. No doubt Megan's possible involvement played its role too.

They rose into the air. Richard had never been in a helicopter, or any kind of small aircraft. He should have felt exhilarated but only felt sick. The noise was terrific. They arced and turned away, travelled at speed towards the *mirage*. If his recollection of Wilhelm's explanation was correct then the land should be immediately underneath, reflected through the haze upon the sky.

The sea barrelled beneath them, pockmarked by patches of ice.

It was bereft of life, as far as he could tell, and the suggestion that there was something within it, a whole new world, seemed farcical. Yet, as they approached the mirage, his hopes began to rise. Green wasn't simply hanging in the sky, but could be seen on the fringes of the sea. The scientists beside him were jabbering and pointing, but he couldn't make out their words. The great bear that was Wilhelm was also gesticulating wildly, Richard's view partially blocked by his frame, so that he only caught glimpses of what was before them.

After another twenty minutes proof appeared in front of his eyes. The helicopter banked, and his sideways view revealed everything. There was a concave opening in the sea, similar, he imagined, to the vortex created by a whirlpool. Yet the sea itself was almost static around that point. A blackness permeated the hole, but as his eyes adjusted he realised there was something inside. Nothing obvious, but land all the same.

A twist of emotions wrung within him, his heart might stop. Finally he gasped and realised he had been holding his breath. Suddenly the machinations of all of this hit him with some force. It wasn't just about Holly any more, or even any of the other children. It was about the rest of the world — and, he wondered, how that might be exploited.

Yet again, was *what* he was seeing what he *was* seeing?

They hovered over the hole for a few minutes, then banked again and headed back to the ship. It was difficult for Richard to judge the size of the opening, certainly no more than a quarter mile across, if that. And there didn't seem any obvious method of egress. How were they going to get down there, if there was a *there* to get down into?

As the helicopter receded he wondered why they hadn't

themselves descended, guessed that they wanted to bring the ship closer before making any decisions. But he was itching to get things moving, and if he could have shouted at Wilhelm over the noise then he would have done so. Could it really be that Holly was down there?

But there was no more time for speculation. Something shot past at an incredible speed, then halted immediately between them and the ship. It was a thin cylindrical object, its silver outline barely visible against the reflected ice and sky, but it was there all the same. The final proof if any was required that something else was out there. That Wilhelm had been right all along.

Within his gloves, Richard's hands were trembling.

WILHELM

ONE

At last! Wilhelm was overjoyed as he exited the helicopter. The flying saucer had accompanied them on their journey to the ship: alongside, above, below, and seemingly able to change those positions in a blink. Whether it was intended to be a display of strength or merely just a quirk he couldn't tell, however the experience felt like swimming with dolphins.

The saucer now floated over them. It was silent, it's method of propulsion unclear. It was also completely still, as if it had been painted on a background of blue sky. Once everyone was out of the helicopter, and the rotor blades slowed to a standstill, the saucer finally descended to a few inches above the deck of the ship. Collectively, everyone held their breath.

After what seemed like minutes, four inhabitants of Hollow Earth stood before them. Wilhelm gasped. They had simply materialised beside the vehicle without a doorway having opened, possibly some elaborate trick. Visually, they were humanoid, wore two-piece tunics, and had shoes on their feet. However they certainly weren't dressed for the cold, and what skin was visible was decidedly a pale shade of green. Wilhelm glanced over to Richard to see if he had noticed, and his expression was clear that he had.

If what had happened so far had been surprising, then none of them were prepared for what followed.

"Wilhelm Hagen," one of them spoke. "Richard Dean, Henry

Wyndham, and John James, can you come with us please? The rest of you will remain here."

His voice had been soft, with an underlying timbre of insistence.

Wilhelm sputtered. "Yes, yes, of course. But how did you know our names?"

There was a smile. "There is little that we don't know. We have to protect the interior and having knowledge is a big part of that."

"May I have your name, you have mine, after all?"

Again, a smile, as though imparting information to a child. "We have no names. We see no need to distinguish between ourselves in that way. Individuality is such a burden, don't you think?"

Wilhelm didn't know what to think. He had waited several years for this moment but it was overwhelming. He had been wrong-footed, needed to exert his influence somehow. And the only way he could do so, of course, was with the members of his party.

"We'll need to take some of our scientists too, of course. We've come a long way and..."

A hand was raised. "I'm sorry to disappoint you Wilhelm, but only the three members of your party I have previously mentioned will be accompanying us on this journey. If necessary, we will also have to refuse *you*. In fact, we are only offering you a place because you were kind enough to bring these men here. You may be influential in your world, and we appreciate your services and acknowledge your wife, however you are not necessary for what is required. Please take this opportunity to visit as a tourist, nothing more."

Wilhelm opened his mouth. Then closed it again.

"Certainly. Then perhaps you will lead the way."

"I'm glad we are in agreement Wilhelm. Before we depart

however we must ask you to leave your recording device on board ship and also your camera. You are the only one of these four carrying such a device, the others are free to board now."

Wilhelm divested himself of his dictaphone and digital camera. He fingered his mobile and shifted it beneath his handkerchief deep in his pocket. Henry, James, and Richard had already stepped up beside the Hollow Earth dwellers. An overall feeling of calm permeated the scene, and he wondered how much of this was influenced by the dwellers themselves.

"If you're wondering, Wilhelm, your mobile phone will not have a signal within Hollow Earth. However, should it be necessary to establish contact with the outer world we may be able to activate that service. Naturally, we will not be expecting any of you to use your phones for any other purpose." He smiled again. "Of course, we will know if you do."

Wilhelm coughed, cleared his throat. "Do we have any reassurances for our safety?"

"You have my word, Wilhelm."

It crossed Wilhelm's mind that the word of a man who had no name might be a promise that would be difficult to prove, however he had no choice. He *had* to get into Hollow Earth. This was the most exhilarating moment of his life, and he could see he would have to push aside pride to gain entry. Once he was there, of course, it would be another matter.

"Finally, before we board, can you give us any indication as to the whereabouts of these men's children, perhaps an assurance..."

Again, he was interrupted. "All in good time, Wilhelm. Besides, there are other ears here, are there not, which are not connected to the four of you we are taking. Information will only be imparted as and when necessary. It is the way we do things here."

"And my ship?"

"It can remain here, at this point. No radio contact should emit whatsoever. If it does, then you may find it won't be here when you return."

This time there wasn't a smile.

Wilhelm turned, gave an order to the captain and crew in the manner that he was accustomed, whilst also promising a bonus on their return should his request be adhered to. It was a formality only, but again a show of authority that he hoped would be conveyed to the dwellers.

Turning back he regarded them a little more closely. The one who had spoken was shorter than the rest, but they were all slim. Their skin looked identical to his, apart from the greenish hue. In fact, they could be normal human beings if it wasn't for the colour, although he would have been hard-pressed to guess their age. They carried an authoritative air suggestive of as many years as him, however certainly they physically looked younger, stronger, more toned.

They were personable as well. Wilhelm found in his line of work that people of that disposition were often hiding another side. What seemed natural on the surface often proved to be just surface, unlike him where what you saw was what you got. If he was to make any inroads here then he had to exploit weaknesses as and when they arose. If he could somehow elevate himself to an ambassador for outer earth then that might be the best role for him. Becoming part of their society itself looked like slipping away.

He nodded his readiness to their *leader*, without names he would have to assign other ways to differentiate between the dwellers. The next thing he knew they were in darkness. Shocked, he realised he was lying down and attempted to rise but found he was strapped in. A voice in his ear told him to lie still.

We are travelling, it said, slightly sibilant. *Keep still, there is no reason to fear.*

Wilhelm waited for his eyes to adjust to the darkness, but it made no difference, he might as well keep them closed. The tone of the voice and the green of their skin reminded him of the myths about lizards infiltrating governments, perpetuated ad nauseam by David Icke and his like. Wilhelm had no truck with New World Order theorists, god knows he had the power to be part of any consortium and to his knowledge nothing like that existed. But until now, he hadn't been one hundred percent sure of the existence of Hollow Earth, had he? Not really. Now there was no doubt at all.

If they were travelling then he couldn't feel it. There was no apparent motion. No noise other than that voice, which he had presumed didn't come from nearby. If only this technology was available on outer earth. Dollar signs advanced across his eyes and before he knew it he was asleep.

TWO

When he woke he found himself on a low-lying platform within some kind of assembly hall. He was no longer strapped down, and movement in the corner of his eye saw Richard rise from a similar bed. He rubbed the back of his neck. Had he been drugged? No doubt they were within Hollow Earth and the nature of their journey had been withheld from them. That was to be expected, but again he felt some of his authority had been stripped away.

If they knew his name, then they knew who he was. He had hoped to be treated with a little more dignity.

Sitting up, then rising to his feet, he looked about him. The room appeared to be made of glass, but it could equally have been a fluorine − based plastice. The outside of the building on three walls was clearly visible − bare brown rock suggested it had been hewn into the natural environment. On the third wall, before which sat members of what he presumed were a council, information scrolled back and forth across a giant screen. He couldn't make out exactly what it was, but presumed it certainly wasn't advertising.

The room was populated with at least a hundred denizens of Hollow Earth. All of them were dressed similarly to those who had welcomed them on the ship, although gradations of colour might have differentiated rank. He couldn't be sure that the *leader* he had met was there, several people were extremely similar and thoughts of limitations of the genetic line underground crossed his mind. Nevertheless, here they were, and subject to public attention. As Henry also rose from his platform and joined the three of them in stance, Wilhelm stood forwards a little, making himself the centre of attention. He waited patiently for a response.

"Let us tell you a little about our history."

Wilhelm looked around for the speaker, but the sound seemed to be coming from all points simultaneously.

"Contrary to popular above ground opinion this is not the Garden of Eden, the location of that can be found at Qurna in Iraq, although, of course, it is entirely mythical. Neither did we arrive here from outer space. To our knowledge, there is no life on other planets − those flying saucers that are sometimes seen are, of course, *our* machines. No, simply we were *once* you. Our paths diverged several thousands of years ago, and since that point our technology and our knowledge — particularly over the past several hundred years — has surpassed yours. We choose to keep ourselves hidden because we see no need to interact. Do you seek to interact with other species? Indeed, you don't even interact very well with yourselves.

"In addition, we haven't exploited our natural resources in the same way that you do. Our energy systems are self-sufficient, our livestock and food supplies too. Of course, we monitor what you do because it can impact on us. And where necessary, we intervene."

There was a pause. Wilhelm was unsure whether to speak, what was expected of them. "It sounds idyllic," he said; simply to fill the space.

"Yes, it is."

Again, that pause. Wilhelm was about to speak again, but then Richard did so, beside him.

"However idyllic it might be, I'm sure you know the reason that we're here. The three of us have come for our daughters. With the greatest respect, we would rather not delay matters unnecessarily. Do you know where they are?"

Wilhelm could hear Henry and John murmuring their assent.

Again, the dissociated voice: "We are aware of that situation. Firstly there are protocols here that need to be observed before we continue."

"Fuck the protocols mate, we want our daughters back."

Wilhelm started at John's outburst. He turned around and intended to restrain him, but the release of tension seemed to have done the trick, and John had already become subdued. He needed to take control again, and did so.

"Please forgive my colleague, but you can understand the stresses involved in this situation. We will do whatever you wish to resolve this matter, and hopefully spend some time with you understanding your ways. However, for the moment, are you able to confirm that these children are safe. You must understand how difficult it is for them."

"The children are safe."

"How can you know that?" shouted Henry.

"You will have to take our word."

"Are we guests or prisoners," mumbled Richard.

"Ssssh," whispered Wilhelm, "let me handle this."

He turned again and addressed the crowd. "We are grateful to you for alleviating our concerns. Please proceed with your protocols so we can draw this matter to a conclusion."

Privately, Wilhelm wondered how they could be so sure if they weren't the captors themselves, but he had to remain on their good side. He didn't have a missing child, after all.

"Our history hasn't always been as idyllic as it might appear. Several hundred years ago we split into different factions. As you know, we have no names, but through your research Wilhelm you will no doubt be aware of the Tero and the Dero. These were names assigned to us after an unfortunate security leak…"

Wilhelm could almost detect a sense of humour in the voice.

"… Which we were unable to control. Nevertheless, the problem remained. A source of energy here would be referred to as magic in your world, and we took precautions to control the Dero through that magic. These would be the rituals that your wives practice. We have found the female members of society more prone to channelling magic, hence the function of that genetic line. I'm sure you have worked this out already."

Wilhelm nodded. "It was becoming obvious to us, yes."

"Unfortunately it seems the Dero are circumnavigating that power, manipulating it to their advantage. We have taken precautions to protect our women, but through historical research became aware of Agnes — as you called her — and her disappearance into your world. The Dero also discovered this information. You can understand the importance of maintaining these rituals. The Dero aren't quite as placid as us."

Wilhelm nodded. "From reports I understand they can be quite brutal."

"You would understand correctly. However, we have disabled them and retrieved your children. It is simply a matter of handing them back."

"The situation has been resolved?"

"Exactly."

"May we see them?"

"They are in another place at the moment, several of your miles from here. We will take you there, of course."

"And this problem with the Dero, has that been resolved?"

"It only becomes your business when we cannot control it."

Wilhelm paused. His desire to know more felt like a physical force pushing out of his body, but he was wary of saying anything which could be taken the wrong way. Undoubtedly, the Tero held all the cards underground. He would have to create a need for himself to know more, in order for them to need him in turn.

"We will give you chaperones for the journey, those of us who met you on your ship. I am sure you will be pleased to be reunited with your children."

Wilhelm nodded. "My companions will, of course, be overjoyed, but I myself have no child here, as you know. May I be allowed to stay awhile with you people, in order to learn more about your way of life?"

There was no discernible pause, no obvious discussion preceding the next statement.

"You will be required to journey with your companions, Wilhelm Hagen. You see, the situation has moved on since we took you underground. Your wives are with us too."

Wilhelm started. *Megan is here?*

"But, how could they be? How could they have come here so quickly?"

"As we have already said, Wilhelm Hagen, their location is in another place. Plus, many days have passed since you left the ship. Nine, in fact, of your days."

Wilhelm's legs weakened. Surely this couldn't be correct? They had only been within the flying saucer for a few moments. Was this some kind of trickery? Beside him he also heard gasps from the others, confirming their fears were the same.

"Forgive us for not imparting this knowledge sooner," said the voice. "It was not considered necessary."

Wilhelm looked around at the sea of faces. He suddenly had a feeling all was not as it seemed. The disembodied voice reminded him of the Wizard of Oz. Who was really in charge here, what was the truth? The more he thought about it, the less he really knew.

THREE

Wilhelm ran a hand through his thinning hair. After their audience with the denizens of Hollow Earth they had been escorted down a nondescript corridor towards a room where they were told to freshen up in readiness for their journey. It was a small apartment, not much more than a basic hotel room, although it lacked a television and most of the other comforts that might be found in such a room. The bed was a double, freshly made. But that was it.

After they had been inside fifteen minutes, had splashed water on their faces, and exchanged a few words, they realised they had been locked in.

"Jesus!" John banged on the door a couple of times, then started pacing the room. Henry sat on the bed, holding his head in his hands. When Wilhelm looked at Richard he could tell he was expected to say something.

Wilhelm fingered his mobile, checked the time. It was 6:21pm and the date tallied with the nine day delay that had been mentioned.

"What now?" said Richard.

"We sit and wait." Wilhelm answered quickly, authoritatively. "We can't do much else."

"Why are we locked in?" Henry spoke from the bed, already defeated.

"Presumably they don't want us poking around. They must be highly protective of their society. We're lucky to be here, many others have failed."

Richard spoke slowly. "What I don't understand is why they needed us. And why so much time has passed. Are our wives really here?"

Wilhelm shrugged. "You know just as much as me."

"Listen," John said, "I've seen stuff like this on the telly and it don't add up, does it? We're their prisoners, aren't we? If our wives and children are safe, then we don't want to be mucking about here overnight. We want to be with them."

"I think we just have to respect that things are done differently here."

"But why? We ain't done nothing wrong. Why lock us up. I don't trust them. I don't trust the lot of them."

John fell silent, stopped pacing, and sat on a chair in the corner of the room. "Another thing," he said suddenly, "there ain't no windows in this room neither."

It was true: no window, no door other than the one they had come through, no external means of communication. Their phones had no signal either.

Wilhelm sighed. The mood had turned defeatist too soon. He had to keep it positive. "Well, either way, we can't do anything before we're called. How about we get some rest until that happens?"

It was a poor suggestion, Wilhelm knew it. None of them were sufficiently at ease to rest or sleep, and there was little they could do besides it. But he didn't want to think the worst. They could analyse the situation all night and be no closer to the truth. Until the door opened again, they were prisoners of the mind as well as of the body.

He thought over what he had seen so far of Hollow Earth. Apart from the chamber where they had their audience, and the interlinking corridors leading to this room which had no distinguishing features, they had seen nothing of the interior of the earth. It was incredibly frustrating, and again he felt he needed to assert some control. But what could he offer these people: information, knowledge, money? Surely they required none of it. Perhaps he should just ask them outright about the possibility of extending life.

Because, that was why he was here, wasn't it. Not to rescue children or save the planet, but to perpetuate his own existence.

And he was unashamed of that. What he didn't need was the others to spoil the relations and muddy that path. His role now was to placate, advise, and ensure they didn't mess anything up.

He spoke again: "We've got to remember that under here they are in control. We're subject to their rules. Imagine, for a moment, that we were above ground. That your children were abducted and taken abroad. You would expect to abide by that country's law, and respect their systems to facilitate a result. We have to do that here. We can't jeopardise anything, especially as we don't know the situation. That would be my advice."

"Yes," said Henry, but in another country we would approach our embassy. We would have an ambassador."

Wilhelm stood tall, breathed in and puffed out his chest. "*I* am your ambassador," he said.

FOUR

In reality, that assertion was short-lived. After another hour the door opened and Wilhelm had been called for. He nodded to the others reassuringly, put his finger to his lips to halt their protestations, and then quickly left the room in the company of one of the denizens. The door was locked behind him with the others remaining inside.

After he had been removed from his companions Wilhelm returned down the same corridor towards the main chamber. No reason had been stated as to why he had been singled out, although he imagined it was because they saw worth in him, rather than that he had no children here.

The dweller who led the way seemed to be the same who had

met them on the ship. Wilhelm was bursting with questions, but he didn't want to be impetuous and knew he had to bide his time. These people didn't need to be rushed, that was evident. All would be revealed when they decided, not him.

As before, a sea of faces confronted him in the chamber, and he stood surrounded by them. Again, a voice sounded which was difficult to pinpoint in origin.

"Wilhelm Hagen, do you know why we have brought you here?"

He cleared his throat. "I'm hoping it is for business, of course. I have many skills, many contacts in the outer world. And I am hungry for knowledge. I learn fast and I keep my confidences. I am sure I can bring a lot to..."

He was halted by high-pitched laughter. "Wilhelm, this is not a job interview. You do not have to prove your worth to us."

The green-skinned dweller who had been his guide stepped to one side. Suddenly, Wilhelm noticed there was a microphone attached to his uniform. No doubt it was he who had been speaking, his voice projected as though coming from the crowd. But then, the crowd…

As he watched, five figures detached themselves from the multitudes, stood up, and carefully made their way down the aisles towards him. All of them were smiling, as though he had partaken of some secret joke. Their faces were not green, and when he turned back to the speaker he found him scrubbing his face with a wet wipe. Green tincture stained the material. Wilhelm shook his head, struggling to believe his eyes.

"What is this?"

"Wilhelm Hagen," said one of the men who now stood before him. "Please excuse our little game. It has been necessary from time to time in our history to pretend we are other than who we say we are. But rest assured, the journey for you is only just beginning. If you desire, you can be part of our success."

"But who are you? And where am I?"

"The latter, first. You are not within Hollow Earth. That's a skin we shed many a year ago. Of course, it has great historical significance containing numerous interesting and necessary relics, and the entrance you viewed is certainly passable, but it is outmoded, outdated. Nowadays we live within your world. Currently, we're in California, USA."

That smile, again. Wilhelm wasn't sure whether it was friendly or contained hidden malice.

"As for who we are? Descendents of Hollow Earth, of course. We are few in number, the war we fought saw to that, but our remainder swiftly rose to prominence within your society over the past three hundred years. You will find us in the higher echelons of your governments and priesthoods, capitalists and communists. Our line has spread outwards like a net, capturing the hearts and souls of humanity. We are shortly to be everything we wanted to be."

"And you have a role for me?"

"We cannot do everything alone. Although we have power and influence beyond your wildest imaginings, we still find key human individuals a necessity."

Wilhelm paused. Could he believe this? These men could be from any Western government, shielding him from the true nature of Hollow Earth.

As if his thoughts had been read, the dweller spoke again.

"Wilhelm Hagen, you may join us. We have access to certain

materials which will lengthen your lifespan. Surely that is reward enough for joining the ranks of the Dero."

"The *Dero*?"

"Well, to use the vernacular. You know your research. It is as good a name as any."

"But, the Dero," Wilhelm struggled, tried to find a diplomatic way to voice what he was thinking.

"In your terminology...we are bastards. But we are powerful bastards who have a very long life span. Who do you choose Wilhelm, God or the Devil?"

A light suddenly illuminated the room. Outside of the darkness which had shrouded the corners Wilhelm could now see the edges of the set. The structure was propped by wooden beams, and the empty spaces where these *men* had been sitting were surrounded by seats occupied by mannequins. The illusion of a great hall, a stately location filled by hundreds, was exposed as a conference room containing six individuals.

Wilhelm held his ground, feigned no surprise. "To make that choice, I would need to know some answers," he said. Although he knew that his choice was made.

"Fire away."

"The green colour, which your colleague removed just now..."

"Necessary to convince you. The diet of our ancestors was such that it caused an uncommon type of anaemia. This anaemia is known as chlorosis — or 'green sickness' — named for the greenish tinge of the skin. Since we have left Hollow Earth and become part of your world, this colour has evolved out of us. Just as it did with the girl you know as Agnes. Of course, legends are legends and need to remain so. Green is the colour of balance and harmony, but also that of jealousy and indifference. And of course, lizards are green, are they not?"

The reference was not lost on Wilhelm, but he chose to discount it. "This I understand, but if you are the Dero then what is your connection to the descendants of Agnes."

Another smile. "The answer, I believe, will determine your allegiance. Is it the case that the rituals performed were to protect them from us, or is it that the rituals protected us from them?"

Wilhelm's head was pounding. How could he answer? "But for me this can be no more than conjecture. I have bits and pieces of research, conflicting theories of Eden and Hell, flying saucers and trolls, good versus evil. Even yourselves have appropriated the names Dero and Tero, possibly only to confuse or confound me. And the world cannot so easily be divided into moral realms. Good and bad pervades each of them equally. No doubt the answer is that the rituals protected them from you, but the necessity of that protection is unknown to me."

"A confusing answer, which is only to be expected. There is magic underground, and those girls could harness it. They need to be stopped if we are to achieve all we want."

"And that would be?"

"Something for you to discover if you join us on this journey."

Wilhelm shook his head to clear his muddled thoughts. It was too much to take in, he had been handed a concept as fact in its entirety rather than by learning it piecemeal. What did they expect him to say?

"Putting it bluntly, Wilhelm, that line of misplaced magic needs to stop right now. It pertains to old Gods, those who have been overturned in philosophical and violent battle. The Agnes child slipped out of our world, replicated, and spread a cancer to weaken us — whether by accident or intent, even for us that is a legend we will never fathom. Quite simply, it survives on belief. But without belief, it dissipates. Hence the need to capture the children. What can crush more than losing a child. Surely anyone would question their beliefs at such a time?"

Wilhelm shrugged. He had no direct experience. He only had a wife.

Who, of course, had once been a child.

Could he lose her, if necessary, to achieve what he wanted?

Again, the answer was unbidden.

"Enough of explanations," the Dero suddenly said, a caustic element in his voice breaking into Wilhelm's thoughts. "We have one final ritual to attend to. Then we can put our minds at rest."

They nodded to each other and began to walk away. The Dero who had removed the green colour from his face now looked at Wilhelm humorously.

"We are not always easy to understand, Wilhelm, not by the caprices and morals of your world. But stay with us and you will know great glory."

"And my companions?"

"They have already been taken care of. Come, are you with us or without us? The Unknown needs to become Known."

Wilhelm coughed, nodded, turned a blind eye. He drew himself proud, negated his past, and followed the Dero into an uncertain future.

RICHARD

ONE

Everything had changed since Wilhelm left the room. The balance of power had faltered. Up to that point they had decided on patience, realising they could do and know nothing until they were released. And Wilhelm was authoritative enough a figure to set the tone. However, after he had left they were equals. Two hours after he had left, they were frustrated.

"I thought we were being taken to see our families," said Henry, slumping onto the bed. He checked his mobile signal for the umpteenth time. "Are we ever going to be released?"

The sense of futility increased the longer they were incarcerated.

Richard considered all the events which had led to this point: his incessant investigations into Julia's past, the discovery of the green link, his desire to get her family together. Could these events have actually been the cause of Holly's disappearance? If he were to take everything as fact, then did those with OCD need to be distanced from each other? Had their identities been protected because they were part of a crowd? And so, by making those genetic links, had he been collecting pieces of a puzzle for the Dero to put together. The more he considered it, the greater he believed himself to be the catalyst. And that was almost too much to bear.

Still, his wife had her rituals, as did the other women in the group. That was some comfort at least.

"I'm getting hungry," John said. He rose from the only chair in the room and walked over to the door, putting his ear against it.

"Hear anything?" Richard asked.

"Nothing, mate; nothing." He knocked on the door cautiously, like a first-time salesman. "They've got to let us out of here, haven't they? We can't stay in here all day."

Richard glanced at his watch. They were already into night, and, now John had mentioned it, a gnawing pang of hunger was also festering in his chest. He hadn't eaten that morning, had he? Nor all day. Although, if the Tero were to be believed they had been travelling for nine days. Presumably they would have been fed something. Intravenously? Or had time just been tampered with?

Disorientation, wasn't it. That was what it was about. He began to wonder the truth of the time they had spent underground. Maybe their watches, their mobiles, had been altered. Anything could have happened whilst they were unconscious. He had only the Tero's word that they even were where they appeared to be.

He kept his suspicions inside. This was no place to get frustrated. A bed, a table, one chair. It was less a cheap hotel room and more of a cell. There was a small door containing a toilet and shower off to the left hand side, and a large mirror on one wall. Other than that, nothing. It was a place to go crazy in.

He started as John banged on the door. His fists were clenched, his face was red. "Come on," he shouted, "Come on!"

Tension knotted his stomach. He decided not to intervene. What good would it do other than to turn the three of them into enemies? And he was more than aware of his own position. After Wilhelm, he was the only the reason for John and Henry being here.

He could only wait for Wilhelm to return. Surely the Tero couldn't be angry with them for feeling hungry, tired, and needing answers. However hard John banged on the door.

Yet, a tiny part of himself, deep inside, occupying a place which he would rather not exist, knew that there was worse to come. He couldn't quite *believe*, could he? That was the problem. Julia was alright, she had her rituals, she had her beliefs, and those beliefs would pull her through. But he knew, as far his own destiny was concerned, that it would end here. And it would end here because he didn't believe, he couldn't believe, that all that had happened could possibly be true. He had simply been caught up in it, thrown around as though trapped within a whirlwind, and would fall, broken, to the ground before all was done.

The sound of John banging harder and harder became subsumed in his consciousness. He was on a spiral, and whilst he recognised it he could do nothing. Despair crept into every cell; hopelessness, helplessness. He wasn't cut out for this sort of thing. All the bravado, all the belief that coming here had been for a reason was leaving him.

And as night drew on, with no answer to their calls, that quiet sense of desperation became further embedded in his heart.

TWO

Eventually, they slept. Richard on the floor. Henry on the bed. John, with his bloodied fists, slumped in the chair.

Richard's dreams were infused with demons. Grotesque faces leered into his own, bodies of children were blackened and burned. He searched for Holly amongst the corpses, pulled by the demons until he felt his arms about to snap. They were wearing masks, he realised, some paper, some plastic, some latex. His flailing hands tried to reach out, snatch them from their faces, but when he did manage to gain purchase the masks changed to skin that stretched within his fingers but couldn't be removed.

Laughter echoed in his head, high-pitched, as though from helium. He could see Julia in the distance, sitting cross-legged on the floor in a yoga position. She appeared to be counting. But it was all wrong, his perspective, the numbers. He was cognisant of dreaming, but couldn't wake himself up. A scream caught in his throat, but couldn't be voiced. Then the demons began reaching for his own face, pulling off *his* mask. But he wasn't wearing one, and their claws tore at his skin.

He woke up, sobbing. The room was bright in contrast — they had found no means of turning off the lights, and in any event none of them wanted to be plunged into darkness. The others were still asleep, their situation was the same. Beads of sweat populated his forehead, gained momentum, and ran over his face. When he tried to sit, he found he couldn't. The strength in his body was all but gone.

The confirmation that he had been dreaming proved of little solace. He was being hammered, fashioned into the man that he knew he had always been. He was fundamentally weak, a cipher, and now was being used. More so than yesterday, he believed it was his own doing which was his undoing. That if he hadn't meddled with Julia's birth line then nothing would have happened. He had empowered the Dero — or whatever they were called. And the Tero, those who held him now? Well, who were they after all? Certainly not the benign entities that Wilhelm had led them to believe.

Richard had no God. But he hauled himself to his knees, planted his hands together, and prayed.

And, like the weak man he was, he prayed for himself first, then for Holly, and then for Julia and Poppy.

After he had finished, he leant with his back to the wall, waiting for the others to wake. Bloody handprints stained the white door. He could only guess what had happened to Wilhelm. He could only guess what would happen to him.

However impossible, he had to keep a low profile. He didn't want John's hands battering him, blaming him, and seeking recourse to the only outlet for his frustration.

Say little, and don't say it often. Curl up on the floor. Head shielded to avoid the blows. Back in the playground.

When he sobbed, he rocked.

THREE

As it happened, there was no violence.

Over the succeeding days, each of them withdrew. Any consolation was to be found inside themselves rather than with each other.

After his initial fury John was a broken man. Effectively castrated, the withdrawal of any ability to affect their situation had beaten him. They no longer spoke. There was no malice between them. He retired to the bathroom and closed the door. Once Richard had tried to open it to find it locked. Occasionally he heard the shower run, but despite his dehydration he had no perception of thirst.

After three or four days their mobiles lost their charge. Within the room day or night was interchangeable. Wristwatches remained unwound, although staring at the faces occasionally precipitated movement.

A delusion of time passing that tormented them.

Hallucinations came aplenty. Unlike his dreams, Richard's imaginings were devoid of demons. Instead, joyful events replayed in his head, granted him worth as a father, re-established his faith. Prayers came to him regularly. Once he believed Holly was sitting on the chair in the corner, but his movements were too difficult to reach her, his cracked skin as tender as sunburn. Even the act of swallowing became unbearably painful. Not that there was anything to swallow, including saliva.

Much later, Richard realised Henry had died. His apathy had increased to the extent that interaction with his surroundings had diminished. Only occasionally would he recognise the door, perceive the fact that it might open. Sometimes, when he was lucid, the door *did* open and he saw his family, but he made no effort to rise and embrace these phantoms.

Only in the vestiges of his memory could they be together any longer.

Then, even that, was gone.

JULIA

ONE

She sighed. The days of rituals were taking their toll and there was no end in sight. Initially they had felt empowered, the circle of life elevated them, the interconnectivity lifted their spirits, gave the sensation of control. But, after a few days had passed, and despite being joined by more numbers, that euphoria had waned. Now, three days without any contact with Richard, worry was her underlying emotion.

In addition to the group she practised her rituals privately, but a sense of desperation, of sheer loneliness, bled into them, tainted them. Poppy's needs fractured her routines, and Holly's absence ate at her soul.

She had been unable to establish why contact with Richard had ceased. They had been exchanging radio messages once a day, but those had been initiated through Wilhelm. She had no way of contacting him direct. She hadn't been able to reach his mobile for some time.

It was a cliché, but without him she realised how much he was missed. He was an anchor. He grounded her. In her rituals she had protected him as part of her family, but without him or Holly her purpose was lessened, not strengthened. It called her beliefs into doubt, made a mockery of them. Like a snake eating its own tail his absence subsumed her, defeated her rituals before she had even begun.

However, if at times she felt defeatist she didn't show this to the others. There were now fifty of her ancestors staying at nearby B&B's and hotels. The rituals continued twenty-four hours a day. There was always a group incanting. As now, murmurs rose through the floorboards to where she sat in Poppy's room, yet it wasn't comforting. Today it seemed futile.

A black mass of despair had descended over her during the night. She had held onto the belief that Holly would return, but Richard's absence meant she needed to believe in both. Her rituals were divided into three separate pleas. One for Holly, one for Richard, one for Poppy. She couldn't maintain the intensity, certainly without seeing — or anticipating — a result.

Results were working against them. More children had disappeared. This was evident from email, and latterly phone calls, word of mouth. But it wasn't limited to children. Megan had also vanished. Julia had contacted her hotel but she hadn't checked out. Communications from others who weren't childbearing had also begun to cease. It was though they were being collected, siphoned off, possibly deleted.

Of course, she knew why they were being taken. If there was no bloodline to pass the rituals on, then the rituals couldn't be perpetuated. And it was also crueller than that. She could have been taken, couldn't she, and the rituals safeguarding her family would have stopped dead. But she needed to be broken, to be punished; that was the reason she came to for Holly's abduction.

Dreams carried her forwards. For the past two nights she had night visions of St Martins Church, the conical roof open to a cloudless yet starless sky. The importance of this building was inherent, whether through magic or tradition it was at the heart of everything she did. The exact nature of its religion eluded her attempts to understand, yet it was omnipresent, both pervaded and informed her rituals. Now, when she was counting, the church was her focus. It was then, and only then, that safety seemed possible.

There were footsteps on the stairs. She instinctively looked over to Poppy in her cot, sleeping quietly. There was a soft knock and Ann opened the door. Her face was drawn, worried. Julia wondered how her own face would appear to an outsider. She barely paid attention to herself in the mirror, although she knew normality would soon begin to reassert itself as, eventually, it always did.

"Are you ok?"

It was her voice, asking Ann. Julia felt the stronger of the two recently, and that knowledge bit her insides as she knew how weak she was underneath her façade.

"I'm fine, but it's so difficult, isn't it, working in isolation of our effects? I know we've always done it, that it's been essential, in fact. But now we're in number I feel we should see results. And there's nothing, is there; no confirmation, no indication, no consequences. I know we felt something once, when we first worked in unison, but it's dissipating, and I don't know if it's our power or just our belief."

Julia nodded. "I don't know either. I just know we have to keep going."

"But how do we know it's successful? Other children have disappeared. It's not working, is it? It just isn't working."

Julia rose from the bed and wrapped her arms around Ann. She tried to give as much comfort as she could, but what were her real emotions. Helplessness, empathy, solidarity…but also a large dose of anger and frustration. Giving up was losing, wasn't it, the belief in their hearts, in their rituals, to the extent that they became meaningless — going through the motions with no expectations.

And if that happened, then the power in their rituals was gone. And with it, hope.

TWO

They were in the middle of another ritual, Julia's mind focussed on the conical church, on the energy she believed it contained.

One. One two three. Two. One two three. Three. One two three...

The numbers escalated in intensity, their voices raised as one. She imagined Holly, safe and back home, playing with Poppy; Richard sat with his back to her on the computer — how she wished she could see *that* again.

Within the ritual, she slipped further into that fantasy. She daydreamed of a world where the rituals weren't necessary. They bound her as much as they supported her. Wouldn't it be joy to abandon them altogether, safe in the knowledge that their magic was no longer required as their enemies had been defeated. To be able to sluice away those constraints, those late nights, the frustration of maintaining the positions of her figurines. Even now, she made sure they were undisturbed. Following the night of Holly's departure she kept a careful eye for any changes. For anything that might signal another shift in the world. Even though the combined ritual had supplanted the others, the absence of routine was both a blessing and a curse.

Yet, to be without those worries completely. To be like the masses, those not descended from the green children, who went about their daily lives with no pressing commitments. Certainly they had their worries, were protective towards their families, but they didn't have the burden. A burden where she could no longer validate her reasoning.

A flash of anger spread across her mind like the beginnings of a stroke. This was her mother's fault, and her mother's and her mother's and her mother's and her mother's and God knew how many generations until that girl had exited the earth. And then, how far back? And when it was telescoped, when it brought everyone together through that ritual, all those generations, why should she be expected to carry it on. Why should *she* have that burden? It was a mantle which she hadn't asked for and which wasn't working.

She became aware of quieting voices around her. Then, quite shocked, she realised she'd stopped counting.

She glanced at the clock. Time hadn't run out, even if *she* had stopped they should have continued. But she was the focal point, the one they looked up to. That was Richard's doing. Briefly, again, a flash of anger erupted over his role. Why couldn't she be left alone?

"Are you ok?"

Ann had broken the circle to sit with her. She glanced around at the faces of others, there were no accusations, they all looked as tired as she felt.

She nodded. Then broke: "I just can't do this any more."

Tears streamed down her face, all the pent up frustration coursed out of her. And as she sobbed, she became aware of Ann sobbing, then the others, until the room was filled with the sound of wailing mothers, desperate for their children, dissected of the belief that they could do anything about it.

THREE

They had agreed to abandon the rituals until the following day. Julia felt a fool, but her emotions were shot to pieces. How could she possibly hold it together? For once, the break might do some good.

Ann had discretely left the house, as had the other women. A sense of desolation hung over them. She knew that many would rather be at home practising their individual rituals, that their sudden familial bond seemed forced rather than genuine. Had the bubble burst? And if so, what of Richard and Holly.

She lay on her bed, Poppy asleep on her stomach. The baby's warmth seeped into her, their heartbeats in unison. Life seemed so precious, so fragile. It wasn't fair that it could be taken away so easily. It negated the beauty of existence itself. Whatever steps were put in place to safeguard a life, eventually they were chipped away. Whether through old age, illness, accident, ultimately it came down to nothing. Poppy's weight on her chest suddenly felt like an unbearable pressure, a stifling responsibility. How could she have ever brought children into this world?

She considered her green heritage, but what did she know of it? Nothing. Even the sudden accumulation of family couldn't link her in time and space. She was a drifter, and whereas her rituals had been her anchor now they were a canker, binding her to a past she didn't understand or feel, and tainting everything she came into contact with.

Not only that, but they would have bound Holly as well. Julia made a promise that if her daughter were recovered then she wouldn't indoctrinate her. It had to stop here. And if Holly wasn't recovered... then Poppy would be spared the pressures.

She sighed. Poppy stirred. Julia eased her from her stomach and laid her onto the bedcovers. Poppy's blue eyes and pale skin seemed so fresh, so innocent. Briefly she considered the greenish hue she had seen on the women's skins the first day they had practised the cumulative rituals. That had been an illusion, wishful thinking, surely. Or was their past hidden just under the surface, how much of them were themselves rather than continuations of what had gone before.

The doorbell rang. She stood up and looked out of the window. Two men in identical black suits could be seen on the porch. In the driveway stood an unmarked car.

That was it. That was all she needed to know.

THE CHILDREN

ONE

Holly gripped the hand of one of the adults. Children outnumbered them here. She was cold and tired. The vegetables she had been given to eat turned her skin green, but she was encouraged to eat them all the same.

The grown-up said her name was Megan. She said she knew her parents. Holly was beyond crying, beyond trusting, but the warm hand in hers somehow made sense.

One night they had played a game. Counting the number of children, counting the number of adults. Megan told her to count in threes, although it was natural for her to do so. Three was a lucky number, wasn't it? There had been three of them in her family until Poppy had come along. Even so, she couldn't count beyond fifty. Megan told her there were eighty. Sixty-three children and seventeen adults.

Holly didn't like the room. It reminded her of a DIY store Daddy had taken her to when they were redecorating her bedroom. Just a large metal chamber with high ceilings and no windows. Only there weren't even the aisles to run and hide behind. Just children sitting and crying and the adults no better. No boys either, which at least was a blessing.

All the grown-ups seemed to do was count. Or to clutch children to their breasts. Megan seemed different from them. True, she also cried, but she kept it inside. If Holly was drawn to her then she didn't know the reason why. Only that there was a kinship, somehow.

When she asked Megan about her parents she had been told they were alright. But even though she knew it was a lie she wasn't angry. Everyone told lies, didn't they. Some lies were just naughtier than others.

She waved at Cassandra who waved back. At the start, it had only been the two of them. They had hugged together as they slept, huddled against the cold. Then as more came they had moved away from each other. She still wasn't sure why. Mummy would have known. She would have talked about bonding.

Megan made marks on the floor which she explained represented days. Holly couldn't see how you could tell day from night unless following each sleep it was a new day. After a while there were more marks on the floor than she could count. Sometimes they seemed too many, and when Megan wasn't looking she scuffed some of them out with bean pods.

But that was in the past. She was gripping Megan's hand now because the doors to the building had opened. In her other hand she sucked on a green bean, its shape in her mouth lending comfort.

As she stood she felt her legs weaken. It made her want to cry but she had to be strong. Maybe she was going to see Mummy and Daddy now. Maybe whatever was happening was about to end.

Wan light seeped into the building, replacing the artificial lights overhead. They moved forwards, into that light. None of them rushed. It was like leaving assembly at school.

Outside of the building the ground was stony and dry. Her bare feet hurt, but she couldn't stop because others were behind her. She was in the middle of the group and too small to see much, but glimpses of fields and a peculiar sky snatched at her vision.

Ahead of them, a conical building pointed upwards. Holly

hadn't seen anything like it at all, yet somehow it was familiar. She felt comforted. They were going inside, weren't they? Maybe that door led out of here.

Megan's soft warm fingers continued to grip her own. Holly realised she wasn't just leading her, she needed her. As the group thinned so they could enter the narrow doorway she became aware of shadowy figures at their sides, directing them as she had seen cows being channelled through metal enclosures at the cattle market. Suddenly, the back of her neck felt cold and she shivered. She clenched Megan's fingers as they entered the building.

The inside was like a church. They each had a seat and faced each other in a circle. She looked up to the roof, but couldn't see the sky through the hole. In the centre of the circle was some kind of structure. She couldn't grasp its meaning but knew it had significance. After all, they were all looking towards it.

Some of the adults started to count. Quietly at first, then with greater intensity, until all of them repeated the same thing.

One. One two three. Two. One two three. Three. One two three.
One. One two three. Two. One two three. Three. One two three.
One. One two three. Two. One two three. Three. One two three.

Megan squeezed her hand, nodded in encouragement, and Holly began copying the grown-ups, found herself saying the words over and again. Warmth spread through her body, a joyous celebration that she couldn't understand, words such as *courage* and *heritage* flashed in her mind although she had no comprehension of their meaning.

It was then, just as she felt connected, that another sense of warmth began to smother the building. Some of the adults jumped up, battered on the walls and the doors. She could hear a crackling, a vivid sensation of terror and hopelessness. Keeping her head down she repeated the counting, coughing quietly, occasionally choking, until all she knew was that she was slipping away, that Megan's hand was no longer in her grasp, and when she fell to the floor and looked up at the roof she saw nothing but fire and smoke spiralling out through the cone.

Oh, and laughter. She heard lots and lots of laughter.

SNOWBOOKS HORROR NOVELLAS

THE BUREAU OF THEM

Cate Gardner

You're not the first to talk to your dead here, the vagrant said. The living always chase after their dead until they come upon their own.

Formed from shadow and dust, ghosts inhabit the abandoned office building, angry at the world that denies them. When Katy sees her deceased boyfriend in the window of the derelict building, she finds a way in, hoping to be reunited. Instead, the dead ignore, the dead do not see and only the monster that is Yarker Ryland has need of her there.

SCOURGE

Gary Fry

Felachnids: a race of mythical creatures that are rumoured to live in the dark Yorkshire countryside.

The yellow eyes, the double-jointed limbs, the heads that turned backwards whenever that was necessary. These creatures, which otherwise resembled humans, appeared to occupy a small village in North Yorkshire called Nathen.

And Lee Parker is determined to track them down.

SNOWBOOKS HORROR NOVELLAS

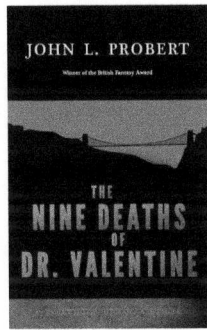

THE NINE DEATHS OF DR VALENTINE

John L Probert

Someone is killing doctors in the style of the murders in Vincent Price movies, leaving the Bristol police baffled. The only man who could possibly be responsible died years ago... or did he... ?

The police in Bristol have been confronted by a series of the most perplexingly elaborate deaths they've ever encountered in all their years of murder enquiries. The only thing which connects them is their seemingly random nature and their sheer outrageousness. As Detective Inspector Longdon and his assistant Sergeant Jenny Newham (with the help of pathologist Dr. Richard Patterson) race against time to find the murderer, they eventually realise that the link which connects the killings is even more bizarre than any of them dared to think...

www.snowbooks.com

www.ingramcontent.com/pod-product-compliance
Ingram Content Group UK Ltd.
Pitfield, Milton Keynes, MK11 3LW, UK
UKHW021323180426
11947UKWH00017B/1393

THE SHINING ONES

BOOK FIVE OF

THE OGMIOS DIRECTIVE

STEVEN SAVILE
AND RICHARD SALTER

Proudly published by Snowbooks

Copyright © 2017 Steven Savile & Richard Salter

Steven Savile and Richard Salter assert the moral right to be identified as the authors of this work.

All rights reserved.

Snowbooks Ltd | email: info@snowbooks.com
www.snowbooks.com.

British Library Cataloguing in Publication Data.
A catalogue record for this book is available from the British Library. Paperback / softback

ISBN: 978-1-911390-26-8

First published March 2017